First Blooms and Second Chances

First Blooms and Second Chances

Nature's Fury and Delights

LEENIE BROWN

LEENIE B BOOKS
HALIFAX

Cover design by Leenie B Books. Images sourced from DepositPhotos and PeriodImages.

ISBNs: paperback 978-1-989410-45-5; ebooks 978-1-989410-46-2 (epub), 978-1-989410-47-9 (mobi)

Contents

Hope at Dawn

Dispelling the Fog

Apple Blossoms and Whispering Hearts

A Lily in Midwinter

Hope at Dawn

Nicholas Sidemore's heart was torn from him a year ago when his offer was refused and the lady he loved sailed away. Today, at dawn, she returns. But has he waited and hoped in vain?

Chapter 1

As the sun slipped below the horizon, leaving its fiery glow resting upon the gently rolling black waters, Nicholas Sidemore spotted the boat for which he had been waiting, bobbing just on the edge of the sea — where the water dropped away and could be seen no longer. His heart raced at the sight of her, and he swallowed the fear that rose inside him as the vessel drew closer. It would not be long now — a few hours or perhaps a day — until he knew his fate.

Using the glow of his lantern to light the way, he carefully picked his way around the rocks lining the shore. Choosing a large one with a smooth top, he sat down. From this vantage point, he could easily see the entrance to the harbour and past it to the sea beyond.

This was where he had sat every night for over

a fortnight waiting for that boat. When three and then four days of waiting had stretched into weeks, he had thought she had chosen not to return; however, there the boat was, three weeks late but with its course obviously set for the bay.

"She's arriving before dawn." A man of slightly smaller stature but with similar features to Nicholas's slid onto the rock next to him. "I hear tell by the other captains that there has been some bad weather. It is probably the cause of her running so late."

Nicholas nodded. That was probably the reason...bad weather. It could not be anything else. It just could not be, for he would not allow his mind to travel down that dark and dreary path. He had spent a year next to it and even been chased down it a time or two by the demons who lurked there. It was not a place he wished to visit again. Therefore, he pushed his doubts aside, propped his elbows onto his knees, and, resting his chin in his hands, watched.

"She's arriving before dawn." His brother's voice broke the silence which had settled in around them. While he repeated exactly what he had said before, Nicholas knew that Jonathan was no longer speaking of the ship.

"And unwed," Jonathan added.

"She did not marry?" Nicholas turned toward his brother, who shook his head in reply. "How do you know?"

"Casselton."

A small flicker of hope flashed in Nicholas's heart. If anyone knew the details of all that was happening in town with its current or past residents, it was Adam Casselton.

However, just as quickly as the hope sprang up in his heart, Nicholas tucked it away. "And how does Casselton know?"

No matter how much Nicholas wanted to hope that she had waited for him, he could not — not yet — for the disappointment would be too great if she had not. When Lady Kathleen Witherfield had left over a year ago with her family, Rupert Dunnaby had joined them, and Nicholas knew that Kathleen's brother and father had both been in favour of a match with Dunnaby. Dunnaby had money and held a promise of more. Unfortunately, Nicholas had only held a promise of riches a year ago, and a promise of wealth was not enough for the likes of the Witherfield men.

"He had a letter from Witherfield that said Dunnaby is not on board the *Mary Ellen*. There was some sort of disagreement, and Dunnaby booked passage on a boat heading to the West Indies. According to Casselton, Witherfield and his sister were not sorry to see him go."

Nicholas drew in a breath and released it slowly. The fear that gripped his heart began to relax its hold, but just slightly. He knew that being unwed and willing to wed him were two very different things.

~*~*~

Kathleen Witherfield pulled her shawl tightly around her shoulders and leaned against the hull of the ship. Overhead, a lantern swayed on its hook, causing shadows to dance about the cabin. Although it was well past midnight and she should be sleeping, she was not. The mixture of excitement and trepidation which swirled within her made sleep an impossibility.

Reaching beneath her pillow, she pulled out a worn letter. Carefully, she unfolded it and smoothed it on her lap. The flickering light from the lantern was poor, but she did not need the light to read what was written on the page. She had read this letter so many times that the words would likely always be a part of her memories.

My dearest Kathleen,

I cannot describe the deep, dark, and dank despair which my heart feels tonight as I pen these words of farewell. They are not words I write willingly. Would that I was able to provide for you in a manner your father deemed acceptable! But, I cannot. I can only promise to strive to do so, but what security is there in that? I do not blame your father for refusing me.

Maybe Nicholas could not blame her father, but she could — and she did! She had been furious at her father's refusal and horrified at his proposed alternative. Rupert Dunnaby was a liar and a cheat, and she had known it almost from their first meeting. Unfortunately, her father and brother had not seen Rupert as she had, at least not in time. She let out a heavy sorrowful sigh and, with a shake of her head to clear the memories of her father, returned to the letter.

I beg of you not to accept Mr. Dunnaby. Give me time to make my fortune. Wait for me, Kathleen. Give me one year to increase my holdings. I shall toil night and day so that when you return, I will be able to provide for you as your father requires. Please do not refuse me this request, for I cannot bear the thought of you with another. I shall look for your answer on the tree behind the church. If I see your locket, I will know you will return to me to retrieve it.

A tear slid down her cheek as her hand moved of its own volition to clasp the locket which hung around her neck. Carefully, she folded the letter and slipped it once again beneath her pillow before snuggling down next to the infant who shared her bed.

Chapter 2

"Heave to!" came the call. Deckhands scurried around above deck, and rigging creaked and groaned.

"Shhh, wee one," Kathleen stroked the head of the baby girl, who rested in her arms and had awoken, as the infant began to fuss. "You will be at your new home soon."

The child had found the journey from Ireland to England to be trying. The constant swaying of the boat had unsettled her, and she had not eaten as she should. What she had eaten had not always stayed with her. She was beginning to look frail.

Kathleen hummed softly, hoping the familiar tune would calm both Aine (awn-ye) and herself. Aine's small fist found its way to her mouth, the suckling action soothing her, and soon, the tune did its work, coaxing both the child and the lady who held her to drift off to sleep.

Not half an hour later, Douglas Witherfield shook his sister's shoulder gently. "We are home, Kathy. We are home."

Kathleen opened her eyes slowly and stretched as much as one could while holding a baby. She gave her brother a half-smile. That word *home* sounded so welcoming, and yet, it also held a great deal of uncertainty.

"All will be well."

It was what her brother had said to her many times during this voyage, and she wished to believe him now just as she did each of the other times he had said it. She knew that he felt keenly the pain of being duped by Rupert Dunnaby. How could he not when the man's perfidious nature had led to the death of their father and uncle? However, seeing the concern in his eyes, she nodded her agreement, though she was less sure he was correct this time than any other time he had repeated the same assurance.

"Is..." She licked her lips and swallowed. "Is he... have you seen who might be on the shore?"

"I have not seen Sidemore, but if Casselton

received my letter, which I am certain he did, then, surely, the gossips have spread the news that you are unwed, and Dunnaby is long gone."

"But that will not ensure he knows I would welcome his suit." That was likely her greatest fear — that Nicholas would not welcome her. If only her locket had remained where she had placed it instead of finding its way back to her by a well-meaning maid. "He has done well for himself, even Papa said so."

Her brother's replying smile was tight. "He has, but if he is not waiting for you, he is an idiot." Douglas opened the door to the cabin and motioned for her to go before him.

She paused in front of him. "Nicholas has no reason to hope." She tried to keep the bitterness from her voice but could not. "When Molly returned my locket, you were quite happy she had."

He caught her by the elbow before she could move away from him. "I was a fool, Kathleen." He turned her back towards him. "I should have trusted you." He unclasped her locket and placed it in his pocket.

Her free hand flew to her throat as she turned toward him. "What are you doing?"

He placed a hand on her shoulder and held her gaze for a moment waiting for her to calm as he often did when she was about to fly into the rafters. Then he turned her toward the ladder which led to the deck. After she had arranged Aine into a position that allowed her to ascend the ladder, he stood close by, ready to assist her if needed. Only when she had begun to climb to the deck above did he answer her question.

"Do you wish him to see you wearing it? He will think you chose to abandon him."

She looked back at her brother, her eyes wide. "I had not thought of that."

She allowed the nursemaid to take Aine from her as she reached the deck, so that she could straighten her skirts. Then, as the child began to fuss once again, she took Aine back and held her close to her heart, cooing to her until she calmed.

Douglas had gained the deck and was standing close behind her, his eyes searching the crowds until he saw the man he sought. Placing a hand on his sister's back, he nudged her forward, so that they might complete the process of disembarking.

Once on shore, he made sure she was on her way to the waiting carriage before pushing his way through the crowds, stopping in front of a man who was watching Kathleen closely.

Douglas took the necklace from his pocket. "Here." He grabbed Sidemore's hand and placed the locket inside it. "This was meant for you." He turned to go back to his sister but thought better of it and added, "A call — as soon as possible — would not be unwelcomed."

"Of course," Nicholas stammered as Witherfield turned and hurried away. Slowly, he opened his hand and lightly ran a finger over the flowers which were etched in the face of the locket. A smile touched his lips for a moment.

"What did Witherfield want?" Jonathan placed a hand on his brother's shoulder.

"He wanted to give me this." Nicholas held out his hand.

"Is that *the* locket? The one that was not left behind the church?"

Nicholas nodded. "Witherfield said it was meant for me." He tucked the necklace into his pocket as he watched the Witherfield coach round the corner and drive out of sight. "However, if I was meant to have it, I am sure there must have been some way in the past year to let me know." He turned to walk toward home. He needed time to think.

His brother stepped in front of him. "You are not going to follow her? You are just going to let her go?"

Nicholas pushed him aside and kept walking. "I do not know what I am going to do." He knew what he wanted to do, but was that what he should do? She had returned, but she had not returned alone. The image of her standing on the deck of the ship with a baby in her arms could not be easily cast aside.

Jonathan, whose legs were not so long as his taller and older brother's were, trotted up beside Nicholas. "Well, you are a daft fool if you do not, at least, make an attempt to win her."

His brother was likely right, but it was not his brother's heart which had been shattered a year ago.

"Witherfield hands you permission to pursue his sister, the only woman to whom you have ever lost your heart," Jonathan continued, "and you *do not know* what you are going to do?"

Nicholas glared at his brother and grabbed him by the arm, dragging him off the path.

"Good day," he tipped his hat to a lady of their acquaintance, who was out on an early morning stroll, following behind her child, who rode in a baby carriage pulled by a small pony and lead by a young groom.

"Mrs. Edger." Jonathan also tipped his hat.

"Keep your voice down," growled Nicholas. "You know my business will be about town in less than an hour if she heard you."

"My apologies, Brother, but you are still a daft fool."

Nicholas sighed. He was going to have to explain a portion of the thoughts going through his mind for his brother to leave him be. "While it is true that Witherfield gave me an opening, have you asked yourself why a man who was so firmly set against me a year ago now nearly throws his sister at me — a sister who arrives back in town unwed and carrying a child, and whose approved suitor has fled after an apparent disagreement with that same disapproving brother?"

He closed his eyes, unwilling to allow his brother to see the full extent of his pain. "Perhaps I am merely good enough to claim her now because no one else will." He turned away, his steps slower and heavier now than they had been a moment ago.

Jonathan grabbed his arm, but Nicholas shrugged him off.

"Go about your business, Jonathan. I need time to think."

"I will be home for tea," Jonathan called to the back of his brother. "See that you are still there."

Nicholas nodded and held up his right hand in acceptance. It was not as if he was going to do something dire. He only needed some time to sort through his thoughts.

Jonathan watched his brother trudge away and shook his head. A woman of Kathleen's rank would not come back to her home in disgrace. She would have remained in Ireland. Hopefully, his brother would come to that conclusion as well. However, just in case he didn't, Jonathan knew what his first order of business was to be today. He needed to find Casselton and some answers.

Chapter 3

The aromas and sounds of morning greeted Jonathan as he stepped into the public house where he knew Casselton always broke his fast. He knew it because he also sought a table in the corner of this particular establishment each morning – the same table at which, with any luck, Casselton would now be sitting.

"Pardon me, sir." A maid, carrying a large platter of bacon and toast in one hand and two mugs of ale in the other, squeezed her way past Jonathan as he doffed his cap.

His stomach rumbled as his eyes roamed over the many patrons in the establishment to his customary corner table.

"Some breakfast for you, sir?" Another maid appeared at his side, standing far closer than necessary and interrupting his survey of the room.

He took a step away. "Just breakfast, Jenny."

She pouted playfully at him. It was the usual greeting of the morning. She always tried to capture his attention, and he always gave her only as much as was needed.

"Have you seen Casselton?"

"I have." She stepped teasingly close once again, looking up at him through her lashes.

He laughed down at her. "Could you point me in his direction and then bring me my breakfast?"

"I'll take you to him." Jack Cotter, the proprietor of the tavern, stood at Jonathan's elbow. "Get his breakfast, Jenny."

Jenny smiled once more at Jonathan before placing a kiss on Jack's cheek. He swatted her backside as she turned to leave. "Impudent woman."

She tossed a saucy grin over her shoulder.

Jonathan laughed. "I never take her flirting seriously, Jack. Your wife is safe from me."

"I've no doubt of that, and Jenny knows it. She only flirts with those like you and Casselton, as neither of you pays her any heed." Jack led Jonathan through the crowded room to his table in the corner. "Casselton, young Sidemore here is looking for you."

Adam Casselton took a drink of his coffee to wash down the piece of toast he had been eating. "Thank you, Jack." He smiled at Jonathan and motioned for him to join him. "It is a happy day for your brother."

"One would have thought." Jonathan nodded his thanks to Jack for the cup of coffee which was placed before him. "However, my brother is an idiot."

Casselton's brows rose in surprise. "Did Witherfield not make certain to let him know he was acceptable as a suitor?" He sat back, the remains of his morning feast forgotten for a moment.

"Witherfield gave him the locket, but no explanation." A plate of food was placed before him.

"*The* locket? The one which was not where it was expected to be a year ago?"

Jonathan nodded as he tucked into his breakfast.

"That was the symbol of her acceptance. What explanation was needed?" Casselton asked.

"Apparently," Jonathan said between bites of bacon, "if you are my brother and if the woman you love's brother, who at one time found you lacking, now gives you permission to court his sister, who has returned after a prolonged stay in Ireland unwed but carrying an infant, it must mean she is in need of rescuing, and you are her only hope."

Casselton's mouth hung open for a full minute before he snapped it shut. "Of all the half-witted notions I have heard him spout — and there have been plenty — that has to be the most asinine!" Casselton threw his napkin down on the table and snatched up his hat. "If Witherfield hears of this, he will be calling him out for questioning Kathleen's virtue."

Jonathan laid a hand on Casselton's arm before the man could rise from his chair. "Finish your food. Nicholas will not speak of it. However, if you could perhaps explain the presence of the child – about which I assume you know." He cocked an eyebrow in question.

"The child is her cousin."

"Truly?"

"Yes."

"It would not be the first time such an explanation has been used," Jonathan cautioned.

"No, you are correct, but in this instance, the child is Lady Kathleen's cousin. Both her aunt and uncle perished. One in childbirth and the other in that fire."

"Then, if you could share such information with Nicholas before the blockhead takes it upon himself to inquire about it from Witherfield, I would be much appreciative. I have no desire to stand as his second or to inherit his fortune in such a fashion."

Casselton huffed and shook his head before finishing off his breakfast. "When you are finished," he said as he wiped his mouth, "perhaps we could pay a call on your brother?"

Jonathan nodded as he sopped up the last of his egg with his toast. "Two bites."

Casselton drummed his fingers on the table as he waited none-too-patiently for Jonathan to finish those two bites and wash it down with the remains of his coffee. Then, snatching up his hat, he hurried toward the door.

"Hold up," Jonathan called as he tossed his money on the table and ran to catch Casselton. "Adam." It was a name he only used when he needed his life-long friend's full attention. The effect was immediate as Casselton stopped and turned to look at him. "Nicholas is at home." He motioned in the opposite direction.

"Nick is at home when there is money to be made?" Casselton's face registered his surprise.

Nicholas Sidemore was not known to leave the running of his bank to his employees without his oversight.

"He is, and if my impression of his mood this morning was correct, he is sitting in the garden staring at the church."

It was where Nicholas had sat every day for two weeks after the Witherfields had left. He had refused to eat more than once a day, and he only at then because Jonathan had begged him to do so. To be perfectly honest, Jonathan had thought his brother was going to purposefully do himself harm during those days. It was why he had promised to be at tea today, for the expression his brother had worn this morning at their parting was so reminiscent of the way he had looked back then.

Casselton drew a deep breath and exhaled it along with much of his frustration as he shook his head. "He is confused."

It was not a question, and so Jonathan made no reply.

"Well, then, I shall tell him a story rather than deliver the lecture he rightfully deserves."

"It would do far more good, my friend."

Together the two turned and started toward the Sidemore residence.

Chapter 4

The Witherfield's carriage drew to a stop in front of a shop on the high street.

"We have servants who can do this, Kathleen."

"Mmm. I know." Kathleen snuggled a sleeping Aine more closely to her. "I am sure they have been working diligently to prepare for our arrival. The apothecary is on our way, and it would be foolish to drive all the way home just to send someone back to do what I can do myself. Foolish and inefficient." She waited for her brother to exit the coach and extend his hand to her. "I would like to be prepared for when Aine wakes. I do not have any tonic remaining."

"We are on dry ground, Kathy. There is no swaying of the ship to make her uneasy."

"Mmm. I still feel the sway, do you not?" Kathleen placed her hand in the crook of his arm. "How long did it take you to no longer feel that sway when we arrived in Ireland. A few days? Or was it weeks?"

Douglas shook his head in resignation. He knew that when his sister was bent on an idea, logic and reasoning were the only hope of changing her mind, and he was well aware that his argument was based on things less noble, such as the longing for a bath and a bed in which he could stretch out fully. There was nothing to be done but to agree with her, and so he did. "Yes, nearly a week."

"She is so frail, Nicholas."

He sighed as he heard the tears that lay behind the softly spoken words. "I know. You are right. We must make sure she has everything she needs. It is as Father and Uncle Barrett would have wished." He ran the back of a finger down the baby's soft cheek. "She is sweet."

Kathleen smiled at him. For all his size and grumbling, he was rather more of a kitten than a lion at times. "She is, and you'll not be spoiling her, Douglas Witherfield."

He laughed, a deep rumbling sound she had not heard much in the past year. "It is good to be home," she said as she stepped into the apothecary shop.

"Oh, and with a wee one on her hip. I thought it strange how quickly they left." Mrs. Edger stood at the counter of the shop. Her back was to the door and, therefore, she had no idea that the object of her tattling had just entered.

Mrs. Benson, the apothecary's wife, cleared her throat in an attempt to silence the woman.

"And then I heard the Sidemore brothers discussing a need for her to be rescued. Well, I can tell you, a woman of such loose morals as to have a child out of wedlock needs rescuing by more than man. And to flaunt ..."

"Loose morals?"

Mrs. Edger spun to see who had spoken to her. "Lady Kathleen. It is good to see you. I trust your travels were not too arduous." Were it not for the bright pink colour that stained the woman's cheeks, Kathleen would have thought her unaffected at having been caught spreading tales.

"Not for us, but our cousin did not fare as well as we did," said Douglas. The mild kitten from befoe was gone, replaced by the gruff and imposing earl. He nodded to Aine. "She needs more of this." He pulled a small bottle from his pocket and handed it to Mrs. Benson.

"So this is your *cousin*?" There was an odd inflection of Mrs. Edger's voice at the word as if she did not believe it to be true.

"Yes. This is Aine Witherfield, daughter of Barrett and Erin Witherfield, my aunt and uncle. You do remember them, do you not? There was quite a scandal when they married, and I know how fond you are of a scandal." A smile tugged at his lips when he heard her gasp. "I assume you have heard of the tragedy we all suffered of late when both Aine's father and my own died?"

Mrs. Edger gave only a small nod of her head to confirm that she had heard.

"I do hope what my sister heard as we entered was not about her," Douglas continued.

Deep red spread across the woman's face. "Of course not, my lord."

"But the lady in need of rescue?" Kathleen wore a particularly tight smile. "It was the Sidemore brothers who were discussing her?" At the woman's nod, she continued, "And how did these gentlemen come to know she was in need of rescuing?"

Mrs. Edger gave a quick glance at Douglas before lowering her gaze to the floor. "I heard one of them mention her brother, my lady."

Douglas watched his sister's shoulders rise and fall three times before she spoke.

"Thank you, Mrs. Edger. I must call at Hazelton House to see what I can do to assist the young lady." She waited until the woman had left before she turned to her brother.

He winced when he saw the thunder in her eyes. "Are we stopping at Hazelton House on the way home?"

"Well, there is a woman in need of rescue, is there not, my lord? Rescuing should not be put off you know."

"Kathleen..."

She held up a hand to stop him. "Not in public, my lord. I will wait for you in the carriage."

He sighed as she left the store. She never called him *my lord* unless she was beyond angry. The ride home was not going to be a pleasant one.

"Would my lord require some headache powder?" Mrs. Benson asked with a knowing smile.

"Yes, Mrs. Benson, I do believe I shall be in need of some."

"She's a good girl, my lord. I'd not believe an ill word spoken of her, and neither would many others."

He smiled at the elderly woman whom he had known since before he was in breeches. "She may be a good girl, but she has a wicked temper."

"Aye, my lord, she's as beautiful and deadly as a summer's day when the clouds roll in." She chuckled as she wrapped his parcel. "Let her blow, and 'twill soon be passed."

"I pray you are right, Mrs. Benson. Thank you." He took the package and headed for the carriage and the waiting storm.

Chapter 5

Nicholas sat with his back resting against the large tree that stood on the top of a small rise in the garden at Hazelton House. Here, with the church in view, he could more easily remember the council he had received from Mr. Baxter.

You must have faith and hope, but above all you must have love, he had said. *Have hope when the skies are grey, have faith when the way is unclear, and have love that is unwavering even in the face of trial.*

He blew out a breath, trying to rid himself of the dark images of the time when Mr. Baxter had spoken those words to him. It was guidance he had needed then and now.

When he had found the hollow in the tree, which overshadowed the grave markers of his relations, empty those many months ago, his heart had been shattered. It was wise counsel such as Mr.

Baxter's, along with the care and companionship of Jonathan and Casselton, that had kept him from being consumed by the dark melancholy which had descended on him.

It was that darkness which currently poked at the edges of his mind and which kept him from running to Witherfield Hall. He leaned his head back against the tree and closed his eyes. Emptiness filled his breast, causing him to clutch the locket in his hand tightly. She had meant this for him. Her brother had said that she had. He blew out a slow breath. Could he find the courage to discover if what her brother said was true?

A shoulder bumped his as someone took a seat next to him. Cracking one eye slightly open, he cast a glance at his friend. "Go away," he grumbled, though he knew that such an order was not about to be heeded.

"In a moment," Casselton said. "I wish to inform you that I am in the market for a wife, and if you do not seek her hand, I will. I stepped aside two years ago when it was obvious she was enamoured with you, but I'll not step aside again if you do not put yourself forward." He made to rise but paused to take one more shot. "Apparently, I have more faith in her than you do. Perhaps I'll not give you a chance."

Nicholas grabbed Casselton's sleeve before he could rise. "No! She will not be yours." Fear much greater than what he had felt up until now grasped his heart and threatened to crush it in its grip. Casselton rarely made empty threats.

"Why should she not be mine? I do not see any others lining up to call on her."

Nicholas released Casselton's sleeve with a shove, sending him sprawling. "Because I love her." He waited for Casselton to scramble from the ground. "Now tell me what you came to tell me. I have somewhere I need to be." No one was going to take Kathleen from him again. She would have to send him away if she did not want him. He would not be prevented from presenting his suit to her by anyone.

Casselton studied the face of his friend. He saw the uncertainty in his eyes and the determination of his mouth. He watched the pronounced rise and fall of his friend's chest and heard the deep drawing of breath. "Then why are you here under this tree instead of dashing after her? And what dark demon possessed you — besides your propensity to find disaster where there is none — to make you think the child you saw was hers?"

"My propensity, as you call it, does not follow logical paths as you well know." Nicholas rose to his feet. "But it is a demon, one that, at times such as these, needs solitude to defeat. Mr. Baxter has taught me many things over the past year." He ran a hand through his hair before rubbing the back of his neck. "I needed to a few moments to remember them."

"And having remembered? What are your plans?" Casselton stood beside him.

"The child is not hers?"

Casselton shook his head. "Do you really think of her as the seducing type?"

"No, but..." Nicholas turned away from his friend. "It does not matter to me if it is hers. I love her. There is nothing which can alter that fact, but I will admit that my heart and mind would rest a bit easier if I knew whose child it was."

Casselton took him by the shoulder and turned him so that they were face to face. "What is the root of your unease? Do you fear that she was abused in some fashion."

Nicholas shrank back at the horror of such a

thought. "No, no. I only wish to know if there was someone she loved."

"Other than you?" Casselton scoffed. His friend truly did not think logically when he was over-wrought about Lady Kathleen. He chuckled as he shook his head. Nicholas Sidemore was logical and analytical to a fault and had been all his life until he had fallen for Kathleen Witherfield. She was the only area in the man's life where logic liked to take a holiday on such a grand scale.

"She refused Dunnaby, and the child is her cousin. The child's mother died shortly after giving birth, and if you'll remember, Barrett Wither-field was killed in that fire."

"The child is her cousin?"

"Yes, a baby girl who has been left an orphan and taken in by her relations."

What a tragic way for a child to begin her life. Of course, Kathleen would take the child and care for her cousin as if she were her own. That was how Kathleen was. She had a capacity for empathy that few possessed. Many had been sorry to see her leave, for they would miss her visits and the help she provided for them, which she said she did on behalf of her father. However, Nicholas was not so certain that the late Earl Witherfield had so great a care for any who were beneath him.

"You still have not told me your plan." Casselton was standing with his arms folded and an easy smile on his lips.

It had been an empty threat. How had he been so fortunate to acquire such a good friend as Adam Casselton?

Nicholas ran the gold chain of the locket between his fingers. "It seems I have a locket to return," he cast one last glance at the church, "and with any luck, she will accept both it and me."

Chapter 6

Kathleen glared at her brother as he handed her down from the carriage. There had been a tirade of words which had greeted him when he had gotten into the carriage at the apothecary's shop. Then when he had insisted that a stop at Hazelton House was not in the best interest of anyone and would *not* be happening, there had been silence — loud, painful, accusing silence.

He held her hand firmly after helping her from the carriage, though she attempted to pull it away.

"Both you and Aine need rest."

Aine was already well on her way to the nursery in the arms of her nurse. Kathleen was not happy about that either. She had wanted to be the one to present Aine's new home to her, but he had intervened. His sister needed to see to herself first, and then, she could look in on their cousin.

"The journey has been arduous." He sighed when she continued to glower at him.

"I only wish for the best for you, Kathy. Whether you believe me or not, it is what I have always sought."

She shrugged but remained silent. The rapid blinking of her eyes tore at his heart. How deeply he had hurt her by not lending his support to Mr. Sidemore's cause! But he had truly thought it a poor match. How could he subject his sister, who had been raised in luxury, to a life such as a man with little income posed? He should have listened to her pleas when she told him that Sidemore was not doomed to being poor. He should have also heeded her loud declaration about never marrying anyone, but most especially not someone he or her father selected.

"I know I have been wrong about things in the past, but of this, I am certain — if you speak to him now while you are tired and angry, you will regret your words, and you know I am right." He tucked her hand into his elbow and held it there as they walked toward the house.

"You know how Sidemore is. He ponders. He analyzes all the sides of a situation before he comes to a decision. It is a process that cannot be rushed. I once thought it a fault, one which would see too many opportunities for advancement pass him by, but I have come to admire the trait."

He shrugged. "I have even tried to emulate it since Father passed. I wish I had seen the good in his methods before we left. Had I evaluated as closely the pleasing manners of that scoundrel Dunnaby, I would never have supported his suit or encouraged his travelling with us."

He took a deep breath. "I am sorry, Kathleen. Had I been more discerning, I might have saved you heartache, and you, Aine, and I might still have our fathers."

"No," she said, breaking her silence. "I knew of Dunnaby's duplicity in his affections for me, but none could have known his full intentions. Not even I thought him capable of attempting to steal Father's money. While he may not have designed Father and Uncle's deaths, I hold him responsible. *Him.*"

She paused as she remembered the night that the fire had started and how her father and uncle had been trapped by falling timber. Dunnaby, whose shoes had been wet from the recent rain, had slipped as he entered the study through the door to the garden. Unfortunately, while stumbling and attempting to regain his footing, his candle had caught a book on fire just before Rupert had hit his head on the corner of the desk. It was a blow that had been hard enough to render him senseless for a few minutes, but still, Dunnaby had been fortunate to escape the inferno to which he had awoken.

He had also been fortunate to receive an opportunity to escape death by sailing for the West Indies. She rested her head against her brother's arm. He had been wise to offer Rupert the chance. As much as she wished Dunnaby dead, she had not wished for the public exposure a trial would have brought.

"It is not for you to bear the full weight of any of it, dear brother. Was not Father as much to blame, if not more so, for my heartache?"

"Yes."

"Is he then to be held accountable for his own death? For if I use your logic, he is."

"I still feel responsible," he whispered. They had reached the steps and knew their discussion of such topics must be reserved until they were once again alone.

"You are not," she replied in an equally soft voice.

Douglas saw her into the house and then, spoke briefly to his butler before turning once again to her.

"I will not argue the point further," he said with a smile. "However, I will take your words as partial forgiveness for your unhappiness while we were away, and perhaps I shall earn complete forgiveness when Sidemore calls on you today?"

"Today?" Her eyebrows rose in surprise. "Did you not just remind me that he needs time to analyze his feelings for me?" A combination of hurt and anger coloured her words.

He drew her down the hall toward the stairs. "It seems I am wrong again, dear sister."

Her brows furrowed, and she wore a scowl.

He laughed at her expression and kissed her softly on the forehead. "I am wrong, my dear sister, for the man awaits me in my study. I shall be giving him my blessing. The decision will be, as it should have always been, entirely yours. Now, go freshen yourself. "

He turned her toward the stairs but pulled her back so he could whisper in her ear. "And do try to wash away some of your anger. Your happiness may depend upon it."

Chapter 7

Half an hour later, after she had washed, changed into a new dress, restyled her hair, and taken a quick peek into the nursery to see that Aine was contentedly lying in her bed playing with a rattle, Kathleen found herself standing at the door to the sitting room.

Nicholas stood looking out the window. The morning light cast a glow around him. She rested a hand on her rapidly beating heart in an attempt to slow it.

He was here.

She was no watering pot, but tears were threatening to fall as she watched him. His shoulders lifted and lowered as he audibly expelled a breath. He shifted his weight from one foot to another. He swung something around his finger and caught it in his hand before curling his fingers around it in a tight fist.

Taking a deep breath and gathering her thoughts, she entered the room.

"Good morning, Mr. Sidemore." She crossed the room and sat in one of the wingback chairs which were grouped to take in the perspective of the garden. "It is a beautiful morning. I must say I was glad there were no further delays in reaching port, for I was anxious to be home."

He had stilled at her voice and now, turned slowly towards her.

Her breath caught in her chest as she waited to see what his response to her would be. He had come to call on her brother, but to what purpose? Was it the one for which she hoped or were those hopes to be forever dashed?

"Good morning, Lady Kathleen. It is a very fine day." He smiled as he took a seat across from her.

She studied his face. It had grown older in the time she had been away. There were creases near his eyes which had not been there before, but in her opinion, they only added to his handsome features and spoke of the cautious character of the man she loved. It was the same cautiousness that she saw in his eyes now.

"I am glad you came to call. I had intended to stop at Hazelton House on my way home, but my brother would not allow it."

"Your brother told me, and I must apologize." He stood again. The hand he had clasped as he stood near the window slowly opened. "Your brother gave this to me this morning. He said it was meant for me, but he offered no other explanation." He let the locket fall on its chain and dangle there.

"And you assumed that the brother who quite forcefully disapproved of your suit had found a reason to find you acceptable?"

He nodded. "I wish I were not the sort who questions all things and sees disaster where there is none, but I am." He smiled sheepishly at her. "You have every right to be angry with me for having ever thought such a thing about you."

"Good, for I am." A small bit of anger still resided in her, but not as much as she had felt at the apothecary's shop.

Her brother had been wise to make her wait and refresh herself before confronting Nicholas, but, to be honest, having him here with her was too precious a thing to risk losing and was a far greater salve to her fayed emotions than anything else could ever be.

He sighed resignedly and held the locket out to her. "Do you want it back?"

She tipped her head so that she could see his face. "Do you wish me to have it?"

He blinked. "No."

"What if the child had been mine? Would you want me to take it back then?"

"I considered that when I went home this morning." He studied the locket in his hand and smiled. "I do not ever wish for you to have it back until you wear it at our wedding. There is nothing, absolutely nothing, you can do which will ever end my love for you." He held his hand out to her, the locket lying in his palm. "But if you do not wish to accept me, then I would not be able to keep this. It would pain me too much to see it, for it would remind me of the greatest treasure I had ever lost. The choice is yours."

Kathleen ran a finger lightly over the locket before wrapping his fingers around it.

"I have looked at that locket every day for over a year and have been reminded of the love which may have been lost." She looked at him quickly before looking again at his closed hand. "I left it at the church, but my maid returned it to me. I would have sent word to you, but my father would not allow it."

She smiled at him through her tears. "I thought I had no hope. I thought you would think I had rejected your offer and would not wait for me. But you did. You did wait for me." She shook her head as she squeezed his hand more tightly closed around the locket. "I made my choice before I left. I chose you then, and I choose you now. "

"You will marry me?"

She laughed at the uncertainty in his voice. "Most happily, I will marry you."

"Oh, my darling, Kathleen." He stood and pulled her to her feet before wiping a tear away from her eye with the tips of his fingers. "How I have longed for this moment! I have dreamt of it, and, upon waking, I have wept over the loss of it." He drew her into his arms. "But you are truly here, are you not?"

"I am, my love. I am." She delighted in the way he held her so tightly as if he were afraid she would be snatched away from him, or perhaps that was how she was clinging to him.

He pressed a kiss to her hair before loosening his hold on her so that he could look into her eyes. "Do you know what Mr. Baxter would often say to me this past year?"

She shook her head. Their parson was so full of quotes and saying that she was certain she could not pick which he would use.

"He would say 'Weeping endures for the night, my boy, but joy, joy comes in the morning. You must hope for the dawn, for it is coming.' And he was right. My joy sailed into the harbour at dawn today." A smile split his face as the joy of which he spoke washed over his features. He brushed a thumb across her lips. "My hope, my longing, my weeping has turned to joy. I love you, Kathleen Witherfield, and I always will." There was no uncertainty in his voice or his eyes as he held her gaze for a moment before lowering his head and pressing his lips to hers. There was only joy.

Dispelling the Fog

Ever since a scoundrel broke her heart three years ago, Madeline Adcock has been searching in vain for a gentleman to both love and trust. In fact, she has nearly given up hope of ever breaking free of the fog of uncertainty which engulfs her. However, with the help of her brother and his best friend, love just might chase that fog away forever.

Chapter 1

The horizon crept closer while the sun sank in the sky and the shadows of twilight welcomed its misty friend. Together, they would obscure much – houses, roads, stars, and even some of the light of the moon. The light from the lantern hanging in the garden would be scattered and hazy rather than crisp and far-reaching.

Fog brought things close. It shrouded everything with its blanket, leaving nothing unchanged by its presence. It was not unlike how sorrow could envelop those it touched.

Madeline Adcock blew out a breath and watched it join the mist that hung low in the air. The evening was cool, damp, and rather dreary. Such an atmosphere suited her just fine. She did not feel like being anything more than melancholy.

She was done. She could not hold onto a foolish dream any longer.

"I have decided." Her heart raced at her own declaration. While her mind had reconciled itself to a future for which she had not longed, her heart was not so easily convinced of the correctness of her choice.

"You have?" Her brother's arm tensed under her fingers.

"You may choose."

"Are you certain?" Fletcher's somber tone held a touch of disappointment.

"I have had three seasons to attempt to make my choice, and still, I cannot see anyone without thinking about *him*."

Neither she nor her brother would mention the name of the charming cad who, during her first season, had led her to believe that he was more than he was.

She knew she should be grateful that she had not had quite enough money to tempt the fellow to actually marry her, and in a way, she was. Life with such a dissembler would not have been a happy one. Yet, part of her longed for the picture he had painted of a home filled with frivolity and good fortune.

For three seasons now she had attempted to prove to herself that such a portrait was not a fantasy. However, risking her heart to discover if it were attainable was far more difficult than she had ever thought it could be. Her ability to trust had been shattered in the game that scoundrel had played.

"He is but one in a sea of thousands. Not every fellow is going to pretend to be what he is not." Her brother stopped walking down the garden path and turned toward her. "I want you to find someone who loves you as I do – well, a bit more, I suppose," he added with a teasing smile. "And I want you to be equally as smitten with him."

"That is precisely why I have chosen to allow you to pick a husband for me. I trust you." And very few others.

"You forget that I was taken in by him just as much as you were. I did not see him as duplicitous until that announcement appeared in the paper."

Oh, what a wretched day that had been! Madeline had not seen *him* for two weeks. He had not been at any of the soirees she had attended, nor had he sent her a note to say he was going to be gone. Then, on that fateful morning, there was his name in the paper, printed in black letters for all to see and linked with that of another lady. He was married. According to the article in the gossip sheets, his wife was a distant cousin and the heiress to a fortune, which, Madeline discovered later, included an extensive estate. Her ten thousand had paled in comparison to such a situation.

She had seen him once after that. In the park. Happily ensconced in a fine carriage. He had nodded his head in her direction and then kissed the fingers of his wife.

She had nearly fainted dead away, but her brother had been there and had kept her from succumbing to the flurry of emotions that overcame her at the scene. That was how Fletcher was. He was steady and strong. She wrapped her arms around his and rested her head against his shoulder. He would make certain she was safe. He always had.

"I trust you," she said once again.

"Very well, I shall give it consideration and see who I might know and could recommend, and then, once you are married, you can return the favour and help me settle on a bride."

"I thought you were decided. Miss Huntly is so sweet, and you seem fond of her. I even heard you speaking about her to Mr. Portman."

Noah Portman and her brother had been friends for as long as Madeline could remember, and the fact that her brother had spoken of one lady so frequently as he had Miss Huntly, both to her and to his dearest friend, had marked the young lady as a potential sister in Madeline's mind.

"I am nearly decided, but one never knows what might have happened over summer. If I had met her at the beginning of the season instead of at the end..."

Madeline felt the shoulder against which she leaned lift and lower.

"One should not make hasty decisions," he added.

She would not disagree with him on that. She had allowed her heart to be given too easily her first season, and look where that had gotten her. Nowhere worth being, that was for certain.

"What decisions are you making in haste?" a

voice asked from the misty shadows near the low hedge which bordered the garden near the drive.

"Eavesdropping is not polite, Mr. Portman," Madeline replied.

Noah chuckled. "I was not listening on purpose. I just happened to hear. That is not the same as eavesdropping, I will have you know." He pushed his way through a small gap in the hedge.

"We have a gate," Fletcher said.

"Not where I needed it." Noah clapped his hands and then rubbed them together. "Now, with what decisions can I help you?"

Madeline shook her head. "None. I have made my decision."

"Then, Fletcher, explain the situation to me, and I shall give you my best words of wisdom."

Fletcher laughed. "Words of wisdom? Did you get some when you were in town?"

"You wound me!" Noah cried in mock indignation.

"Was your journey good?" Madeline asked, bringing a more serious tone back to the conversation.

"Yes. It was exceptional. My new curricle will be ready in a month's time." He pulled a watch from his pocket. "And, tell me, Miss Adcock, what do you think of this chain?" He dangled it in front of her.

Madeline caught the twirling timepiece, which she knew was one of his prized possessions, and looked closely at the links of gold attached to it. "I think it suits it quite well. It as if they were always meant to be together."

He lifted the watch from her hand and ran a finger over the cover before tucking it back in his pocket. "I thought the same thing. I think Grandfather would have chosen this particular chain. That is why I picked it."

"He would be pleased to see you caring for it so well."

"I thank you." His eyes lingered for a moment on hers before he turned back to her brother. "About the decisions you need to make – do you think we might be able to discuss the particulars inside with a cup of tea or mug of ale?"

"I do not see a need to discuss them at all, but I will not refuse your company," Fletcher answered.

Madeline dropped her brother's arm. "I shall go in ahead of you and see that some ale?" She waited for a nod from her brother before continuing. "Is brought to the small drawing room along with some cheese and rolls or perhaps a pasty."

"Are there any biscuits or cakes?" Noah asked.

"I will see what can be acquired," she assured him.

"You are a blessed angel," he called after her.

Noah had a monstrous sweet tooth. He had often been scolded for eating too many sweets when he was a boy. Not that anyone could stay put out with him for very long. He just had a way about him that made one accept him, faults and all. Her brother was fortunate to have such a friend as Noah Portman.

"Briggs, we would like to have some food brought to the small drawing room." Madeline took off her wrap and folded it over her arm. "Ale for Mr. Portman and Fletcher. A hot toddy for me if there are still some lemons about, and some sort of cheese or meat and bread as well as a few sweets for Mr. Portman." She smiled. "And me," she added in a whisper.

"Right away, miss. May I take your wrap?"

"Thank you, Briggs, but I can see it to my room. If you could have someone make sure the fire has been stirred in the drawing room. The air tonight is damp and chilling."

"Of course, miss."

By the time Madeline had put her wrap in her room, made certain that the moisture in the night air had not done too much damage to her hair, and made her way to the drawing room, Noah and her brother were already settled into chairs next to the fire, which crackled its welcome to her.

"You can feel the seasons changing," Noah commented. "The earth seems to be giving up her warmth much more quickly these days."

"And it is getting dark much sooner," Fletcher agreed.

"I like it." Madeline poked her feet out towards the fire. She loved curling up near the hearth with a blanket and a book in late autumn. She could do without the ice and snow of winter, but she did not mind the need for warmer layers and a fire.

"For now," Fletcher muttered. "You'll have had enough of it before the cold has decided to take its leave of you."

That was true. By Twelfth Night, she would be growing tired of the lack of sunshine. But then, there would be the festivities of the season to keep her entertained. One could not miss the sunshine too much when standing in a ballroom lit by a host of candles or when watching a story acted out on a stage. There were definitely parts of the season which called to Madeline, but then, there was the purpose of the season for single young ladies and gentlemen which caused the candles of that ballroom to glisten far less in Madeline's mind.

"What news is there from town?" Fletcher asked.

Noah shook his head. "Nothing of significance. Your townhouse will be ready for your arrival after Twelfth Night. The paper in the sitting room on the second floor – that one next to Madeline's room which goes with the blue bedroom – had just been finished when I arrived to have a look. I think that there is only the paint in the music room left as far as refreshing of décor is concerned."

"And your apartment?" Fletcher asked.

"It is as is always is. However, I might be giving it up as a townhouse will be more practical once I marry, which I do intend to do at some point. I was told that the lease on the house two doors down from yours may become available, and I should very much like be your neighbour both there and here."

"That would be lovely." Madeline enjoyed having Noah visit, and, when in town, he seemed to be at their townhouse nearly as often as they were, much like he was almost a daily visitor here when they were all in the country. A day without seeing Noah was a day that lacked a certain brightness.

"Do you plan to marry soon?" Fletcher asked.

"Do you?" Noah replied. "I have seen nothing in the paper indicating that Miss Huntly has found a husband." His eyebrows waggled over twinkling eyes.

"That does not mean she has not found a future husband."

As well as being steady and strong, Fletcher was cautious. It had taken him some time to accept the scoundrel who had broken Madeline's heart. There was something that had caused him to pause and only reluctantly give his approval. That was another reason why Madeline trusted him. If she had listened to his misgivings, she never would have found herself as she did now.

"It does offer some hope," Noah countered. "And what about you, Maddie? Are you going to leave us forlorn before the end of this season by finally accepting one of your many suitors?"

Madeline accepted the cup of warm spiced, lemon and whiskey that Noah had retrieved for her from the tray which had been brought in. "That is entirely up to my brother."

Noah, who had turned from her to return to the tray on the table to the left of where they sat, stopped and turned back. "What do you mean?'

"I have decided that Fletcher can choose who I am to marry."

"Fletcher?"

Madeline nodded and sipped her drink.

"The fellow who cannot decide if he does or does not wish to marry the lovely Miss Huntly, who, by the by, he cannot stop speaking about and in whose presence, he becomes oblivious of all else?"

Again, Madeline nodded and took a sip from her cup.

"Do you think that is wise?"

"He cannot do any worse than I have done."

Noah dropped into his chair without a mug of ale or morsel of something sweet. "You should have allowed me to shoot that blackguard."

Fletcher had been angry about what had happened to Madeline, but his anger had been far better contained than Noah's had been when he heard of the ordeal. It was only her begging him not to be foolish which had kept Noah from calling the ne'er-do-well out.

"And see you in chains?" She held his gaze. "I could not abide that. Not even if the man deserved a hole in his shoulder."

Noah smiled. "As long as you know he deserved it and think that I would have been successful, I shall make an effort to be content."

"Thank you." Over the rim of her cup, Madeline returned his smile. If she could find a gentleman like Noah, she would be assured of a happy future. Whoever ended up being his wife would be a fortunate lady. It was too bad he had never paid her any more attention than one does the little sister of a friend. She could have easily been persuaded to love him. She liked him well enough, or, she thought while sighing silently, perhaps even a bit more than well enough.

Chapter 2

"Good day, Miss Adcock." Noah breezed into the sitting room without being announced.

There was no need for announcing such good friends – or so he had told Madeline on each and every occasion when she had commented on it. She had eventually given up reminding him of the way things were normally done, and she had to admit that it did seem foolish to announce his arrival each time he appeared as it was rather frequent. Mr. Portman was more family than neighbour.

"To what do we owe the honor of such an early call?"

"Is it early?" He pulled his watch from his pocket and flipped it open. His lips pursed as he looked up from his study of the watch's face. "It is not early."

Madeline chuckled.

"That was a very good joke," he added as he took a seat near her.

"Thank you." It was not always so easy to catch Noah unaware. He must have a great deal on his mind to have fallen prey to her tease.

"You have made some very good progress on this piece." He bent near to study her work, which caused her to stop stitching so that she would not knock his head by accident. He picked up the picture that lay on the table next to her. "Is that this part?" He pointed to the petals which were falling from the flower.

"Yes, this is the first, and then, there will be another in a slightly darker shade behind it. Right here." Using her finger, she drew where the second petal would go.

"Painting would be faster."

"Perhaps, but I prefer creating pictures with needle and thread."

"It is lovely." He smiled at her as he put her drawing back on the table. "I would be happy to just have that sketch in a frame. You are quite talented." He took a pencil out of his pocket and opened the notebook he carried.

"What are you doing?" She asked as he wrote *artistic but prefers fabric to paint.*

"I do not wish to forget any detail when I describe you to my friend."

"When you do what?" She lifted her eyes from his writing to his face. He did not appear to be jesting with her.

"I have been thinking for a good portion of the night, and as the sun was rising, it became perfectly clear to me that your brother needs help in finding you a suitable husband. You have seen how he had dawdled in securing Miss Gray. Fletcher is wise, but he is not decisive in anything that could be called a rapid fashion."

"It is not a race to see me wed, Mr. Portman."

"Noah," he said with a lifted brow. "Save the Mr. Portman for when you are scolding me or in town."

"I was scolding you."

His lips tipped up into a smirk. "I know. I was attempting to not make it one."

"Have you eaten breakfast?" His hair was not as tidy as it usually was. It looked as if he had been running his hand through it right before squashing it down with his hat. And his jaw bore the signs of having not been shaven.

"I had a cup of coffee and a scone. Why do you ask?"

"You look... well... as if you rushed over here in a great hurry, and I feared you forgot to eat."

He scratched his chin. "You are not entirely incorrect. I was in a hurry to see you." He glanced around the room. "Is Fletcher here? I had meant to see him as well, though I did forget for a moment when I saw you."

"Indeed? Am I so beguiling?" she teased.

He held her gaze for a moment. She could not read the look in his eyes, but it was not one of laughter. "I blame your questioning me about the hour. I have had very little sleep. Such a detail as wishing to see both you *and* your brother is easily knocked from its place when one is tired."

"I apologize. I shall inquire about your sleep before I tease you next time."

He returned her smile before turning his eyes from hers and back to his notebook.

"I think I have thought of a perfect suitor for you." A touch of red crept above his cravat, which was curious as he was not usually one to blush at much of anything.

"What is his name?"

Noah shook his head. "I cannot tell you."

"Will it not be hard for me to know whom to accept if I do not know the gentleman's name?"

He opened his mouth and then closed it again, a pensive look settling on his face. "You have a point. However, I do not think you need to know that now. I should hate for you to pin your dreams on a name and then have it discovered that the gentleman is not unattached or as worthy as he needs to be for you." He patted her arm. "I will tell you his name when it is time."

"Will you tell my brother his name? I would feel much more at ease if I knew Fletcher approved."

"Do you not trust me?"

She tipped her head and studied him. If there was one gentleman in England, other than her brother, whom she would trust with her very deepest secrets, it was Noah Portman. Had he not offered to kill a rogue to avenge her heart?

"It is not that I do not trust you." She blew out a breath. "I find my heart is still rather skittish."

"You should have let me shoot him."

"It would not have removed the damage he did."

Noah scowled. "I suppose you are right."

"I know I am right, but I find it endearing that you would call him out on my behalf."

He grasped her hand. "How could I not?"

The intensity of his tone startled her and caused her heart to long for a gentleman who would declare himself to her in such a serious tone with the same searching look that was in Noah's eyes.

He released her hand as Fletcher entered the room.

"Am I interrupting something?" Fletcher teased.

"Not at all," Noah answered with ease. "I have selected a suitor for Maddie."

Fletcher lowered himself slowly into his chair while giving his friend a questioning look. "Who would that be?"

"He cannot tell me," Madeline replied.

"And why is that?" Fletcher asked Noah.

"I think it best if we approach the arrangements with care." He tipped his notebook away from Madeline and scratched something on a page before ripping it out and handing it to her brother. "Maddie said she would be more comfortable if she knew you approved." He folded the torn page in half and then in half again. His hand appeared to tremble slightly as he extended the note to her brother. "I think I would be more at ease if I knew you approved of this gentleman as well."

"This is to remain a secret?" Fletcher asked.

"I think it best." Noah ran a finger around his cravat as Fletcher unfolded the paper Noah had given him.

"I thought we might begin by listing the things that Madeline would wish for in a husband, and then, if this fellow qualifies, I could write to him and present the idea. We might even be able to have him come for a call before the season, unless you wish to leave it all until after Twelfth Night."

He was babbling unusually fast as if he was excessively nervous.

Fletcher's eyes grew wide as he read the paper in front of him. "Are you certain?"

Why would Noah's suggestion cause Fletcher to look so startled? Madeline turned her gaze back to the seemingly still uneasy Noah, whose jaw clenched as he nodded.

"He seems like a fine fellow."

"I would not disagree with that," Fletcher muttered before tipping his head this way and that as he often did while considering such a thing. "And you truly wish to keep this secret?"

Again, Noah nodded. "For now."

"Do you approve of him?" Madeline asked.

Fletcher chuckled. "I would not deny him a chance to win your affections."

"Then you approve?" Madeline asked again.

"Yes. I think this fellow has a very good chance of making you happy if, once you meet him, you find him to your liking." Fletcher rubbed the back of his neck. "I cannot completely make this decision for you, Maddie. You will have to decide if you wish to accept whomever I recommend."

Madeline nodded her acceptance.

"Then, before Mr. Portman expires," Fletcher continued, "I suggest we get on with creating this list he wishes to make."

Once again, she shifted her attention back to Noah, who she had to admit was looking a bit worse for the wear of waiting.

"Where shall we begin?" she asked him.

"Stature," her brother offered when Noah seemed unable to form a reply. He was acting very strangely today, but then, he had likely never attempted to play matchmaker before.

"Stand up, Portman."

Noah rose to his feet, and Fletcher placed himself next to his friend. "Would you rather a thick fellow like Portman or someone a bit more on the willowy side like me?"

She laughed. "You are not willowy, Fletcher."

"I am not as broad as Noah."

"No, but that is because he is more..." She searched for the correct word. Noah was broad, solid, and strong. But to say he was more muscular than her brother might offend Fletcher. Gentlemen were delicate when it came to some things such as perceived strengths and weaknesses. However, muscular was the only word which came to mind, so she used it. "Muscular – not that you are not equally as strong. It is just that his strength can be seen more readily."

Noah smiled and poked Fletcher with his elbow. Gentlemen were such strange creatures.

"I did not say one was better than the other, Mr. Portman."

He shrugged. "What about height? Do you wish for someone taller than us or shorter?"

Madeline stood and, pushing them apart, placed herself between them. Then, she rested her head, first, on her brother's shoulder and then, against Noah's upper arm. He was not only broader than her brother, but he was also about two inches taller.

"No taller than Noah," she said. "I do not want my head to rest on an elbow." She drew a line from where her head had rested on Noah's shoulder to his chest. My! He was even more solidly built than she had thought. "Yes, my head could rest quite nicely on a gentleman's heart if he is not any taller."

Fletcher's mouth was agape. "Girls think about those things?"

She smiled. "This one does. The rhythm of a heart is a very soothing sound." She looked between them. "What else do you wish to know?"

"Hair colour?" Noah shot a look at Fletcher, who shrugged.

"I suppose it does not really matter what colour his hair is as long as it is not currently grey. I have no desire to marry a gentleman in his dotage."

"What if he does not have any hair?" Fletcher asked.

"Does he have a nicely shaped head? And will he still look good in a hat?" She really did not care about such things, but it was enjoyable causing her brother and Noah to look more and more per-plexed.

"He has hair," Noah answered.

"Do you really look at the shape of a head and how it holds a hat?" her brother asked.

"I notice a lot of things. That is why my sketches are so detailed."

"She is very good at drawing," Noah agreed.

Madeline smiled. "So you have noted. Are you going to write this other information down?"

"Oh, yes. Yes. Your brother distracted me with the standing up thing, and then you..." He rubbed his chest over his heart as he shook his head and picked up his notebook. "Eyes."

"I should like that he has some," Madeline teased. "And I would prefer that both worked."

Noah arched an eyebrow and gave her a look that said he did not appreciate her sarcasm.

"Brown or blue or green or grey or hazel. It really does not matter to me." She pulled in a breath and released it. "As long as when I look into his eyes, I can see that he truly cares for me and would never allow me to be harmed." She held Noah's gaze. He had lovely brown eyes. "Much like I see when I look in Fletcher's eyes." She sighed. "And yours," she added with a small shrug and a smile. The answer seemed to please Noah.

"How do you prefer for him to dress?"

"Not like a fop," Madeline replied, pulling her eyes away from Noah to look at her brother, who had asked the question. "I prefer a sensible man."

"Carriages? Income?" Noah asked.

"He should have an estate which is not in decline, and, of course, the accompanying servants. I think such a gentleman would also have the necessary equipage to transport his wife and family in comfort."

"No broken-down carriages or houses," Noah said with a nod. "More than a maid of all work." He winked at her.

"A great deal more than a maid of all work," she said with a laugh.

"Children." Her brother held up a hand when she opened her mouth to reply. "As in, how many would you wish to have if all things were perfectly in your power to control?"

"An even number and no more than six."

Noah tipped his head. "Why an even number?"

"So that no one is lonely, of course."

He shook his head. "I was never lonely, and I was but one."

"That is because you had Fletcher just as I did."

"I think it is more likely that I am not easily lonely," Noah muttered as he scratched down the numbers two, four, and six on his list.

"That might cover all the essentials," Fletcher said.

"No, it does not," Madeline protested. "You have not asked me about his character or if I wish for him to like dancing or music."

"We already know that you love both dancing and music but not the opera," Noah said. "We also know that you are fond of art, but you do not require others to enjoy it as you do." His brow furrowed. "While I do not think you wish for a stupid fellow, and I assure you this gentleman is not such a person, do you wish for a husband who adores reading as you do?"

She shook her head. "As long as he can read."

"Do you wish for him to read to you? For if you do, then we will have to cross off all those who croak."

"Are you going to match me with a frog, Mr. Portman?"

"Only if he is a prince in disguise," he assured her. "Do you wish for him to read to you?"

"That would be very pleasant I should think, but it is not entirely necessary."

Noah shut his notebook, and Madeline reached for it.

"You have not taken any notes on his character."

Noah pulled the notebook away from her and captured her hand. "He shall not be duplicitous, he will be of the finest character with nary a blemish to his honour, and he will love you as you deserve. Will that suffice?"

His thumb caressed the back of her hand as he spoke, rendering her unable to reply with anything more than a nod of her head.

"Then, I believe we have all we need," Fletcher said, rising. "Portman, I was hoping you would join me for a short ride now that the frost has melted away and the air has grown a trifle warmer than it was this morning when I first thought about riding."

"An excellent idea!" Noah agreed. "And you can go back to your stitching which I so rudely interrupted with my early arrival." He gave her a teasing smile, and with a bow, followed her brother from the room.

Chapter 3

Archery was not something Madeline had spent very much time practising. She preferred rambling through the garden and into the wildwood beyond. However, today, with the sun shining as it was, and with this section of the garden, which was laid to lawn, being so close to the path which led to the stables, archery had seemed the perfect activity in which to take part.

She had been out here for nearly a half-hour already, sending her arrows flying at one target about fifty yards away while standing next to the one she would shoot at when she went to collect her spent arrows. Just as she was preparing to shoot her final arrow, she heard that for which she had been listening — the sound of horses clipping and clopping along the gravel path that wound its way to the stables. Fletcher and Noah had gone riding, and as she turned toward the path, she was delighted to see that it was indeed them returning.

She watched them for a while, her fifth arrow hanging loosely between her fingers. Finally, when Noah spotted her, she waved and then turned back to the target, which was looking rather barren. Two arrows had hit close to the mark, but the other two lay on the ground. Hopefully, now that she no longer needed to look at the path to see if there were approaching riders, this final arrow would end up where she wanted it to go.

"Lift your elbow." Noah called as he swung down from his horse. "Let me show you." He tossed his horse's reins to Fletcher and trotted over to Madeline while her brother took both horses toward the stable.

He waved a finger in the direction of her target. "Show me your stance."

Madeline lifted the bow she had lowered when he had called to her.

"I am going to guide you."

He stepped close enough to her that she could feel his breath on her ear and smell horse and fresh air as it mingled with the spicy fragrance that often hung around him. His arms wrapped around her so that one hand could help her hold the bow while the other grasped her elbow and lifted it to where he thought it should be.

"Now, pull back."

His words tickled her ear in a most delightful way.

"Pull back," he repeated.

Oh! She had forgotten in the wonderfulness of him whispering to her and nearly holding her, that she was supposed to be shooting an arrow. She muttered an apology for woolgathering and dutifully drew her arm back. His hand, which was still holding her elbow, moved with her.

"Look where you want the arrow to go."

She nodded.

"And..." He peeled his hands away from her. "Release."

Her elbow dipped as his hand pulled away, and he put a finger under it to push it skyward. She drew a steadying breath and sent the arrow flying.

"That was close."

She felt bereft of his presence when he stepped away.

"May I have a go?"

He was three long strides ahead of her on his way to the target.

"I can shoot one direction, and you can shoot the other," he called over his shoulder.

It sounded as if he had answered his own inquiry and had given himself permission to join her. However, as it turned out, he was only suggesting what could happen, for three strides later, he stopped and turned toward her with his charming grin firmly in place and asked for permission once again. "What do you say?"

It was not a hard decision, for she would like nothing better than to spend some time doing anything with him. The five days since he had returned from his trip to town had been exceptionally pleasant as he had spent a portion of each day with her and her brother, which was his custom. "Of course, Mr. Portman, you may take a turn."

"You are too kind, Miss Adcock." He sketched a bow and then went about retrieving arrows.

Madeline's eyes watched him as she traversed the last few feet to the target while her mind considered how wonderful it would be if this gentleman to whom Noah had written about her was as lovely as Noah. Her last step stuttered.

When had she started comparing gentlemen to Noah? Had she always done so? No, she was nearly certain she had not. She had compared them to Fletcher and to her father — and, of late, to that scoundrel who had lied to her. Her left brow rose. Perhaps Noah had figured into all that comparing, as she had on more than one occasion wondered if the gentleman she was with would offer to shoot a blackguard for her.

"I will need your bow. I cannot just hurl the arrows at the target."

She shook her head to clear it of her distracting thoughts. "Right. I apologize. I was woolgathering, again. I am very good at it today, it seems," she added with a little laugh.

"You should have told me before I sent my letter, and I could have listed it with your other accomplishments," he teased.

"Have you had a reply?" Ever since he had shown her a copy of the letter he had sent, she had been eager to know if he had received word back from his mysterious friend. She was not so much excited to be courted — that bit actually made her a trifle anxious — but she was as curious as could be to discover who it was that Noah thought would make an excellent husband for her. His letter had been impressive. He had listed things about her that she had no idea he knew.

"It has only been five days," Noah reminded her.

"Does he live a great distance from here?" Surely, if he lived within fifty miles, there could have been some sort of reply by now.

"Not an overly great distance." Noah was twirling the arrow he held in his hand and not looking at her.

"Is something bothering you?"

He blinked and shook his head. "No. Why?"

"I do not know. It seemed as if you do not wish to discuss your friend." She handed him her bow.

He shrugged. "Perhaps I do not want to, and before you ask it, I cannot tell you why."

Her brow furrowed. She did not appreciate all the secrets that were being kept from her. There were several times over the past five days when she had heard Noah and her brother whispering, but they had immediately stopped when she entered the room.

"Why the sigh?" Noah stood ready to release an arrow.

"I do not like secrets."

He made his shot and then turned to her. "I am sorry. It is only for a while longer, and if you must know, I am not fond of keeping secrets from you, which is why I would prefer not to speak of my friend." He held her gaze. "This will not harm our friendship, will it?"

She shook her head. "But I suppose it will eventually affect it. How can it not? I will be married and however far away." She diverted her eyes so that he would not see the tears which had sprung to them at the thought of being separated from him. "And you will marry at some point." She attempted to smile at him when his second arrow had hit the mark.

"I suppose I will." He gave her a questioning look.

Once again, she turned her eyes away from him. "Since you are finding a husband for me, you should tell me what you wish for in a wife, and then, I could find a wife for you."

His third arrow went wide at her comment.

"I... I... I have no need of assistance at present." He seemed uneasy about making the admission.

"You do not? Have you found someone then?"

He puffed out his cheeks and nodded as he released the air slowly. "I may have."

"Who is it?" Her heart was surely going to break, and she was not entirely certain why it felt so.

"Are you well?"

"Yes. I am just surprised to hear you have found a lady. You have hidden it very well."

His eyebrows rose at her sharp tone.

Why oh why were her emotions in such a muddle? Drawing a breath, she willed herself to remain calm. They would both get married someday. That was how things were. It had always been so. The thought had never before caused her to become cross, and there was no need of it now.

"Will you tell me her name or are you afraid doing so might somehow ruin your chances?"

His pained expression was answer enough. So, this was to be another secret that she was not allowed to know.

"Can you tell me about her?"

"Are you certain you wish for me to do so?" he asked.

No. But she also did not want him to not tell her about the fortunate creature who had captured his attention and admiration. So, she nodded.

"Very well." He shot his fourth arrow and prepared to shot the fifth. "I will tell you that she is the most beautiful lady I have ever met. She is about so tall." He held the arrow in his hand level with his chest to indicate his lover's height. "She has eyes that speak volumes, and hair that is often arranged so that a few strands hang loose against her neck just here." He pointed to below his ear.

"That is not unusual. There are many ladies who do that very thing."

"Are there?" He looked genuinely surprised.

Madeline nodded. "Even I do that. Not that it is purposefully done to be alluring, mind you. I just like how it looks."

His lips tipped up into a smile. "So you do."

"What else can you tell me about her? Does she like music?"

"Yes." He pulled his arrow back.

"Dancing?"

"Very much." He released the arrow and watched it fly.

"Painting?"

He paused and tilted his head. "I do not think she prefers it. At least, she has not given me any indication that she does."

"Can she play an instrument?"

He nodded. "And she sings. It is not the sort of voice which would grace a stage, but I find it very pretty."

"Then, she is not perfect?"

He laughed. "Perfection does not exist, but if it did, she would be the picture of it."

Madeline could not help but sigh at such sweet words. What she would not give to be the lady about whom he spoke.

"I think I would like her." It was a most disappointing thought for she truly did not wish to like her. She wanted to be able to find fault and dissuade him from his choice. She gasped. Jealousy?

"Oh, goodness." Her hand flew to the base of her throat. She was jealous of a lady she did not even know.

"Are you well?"

Madeline shook her head. "I am not certain." The world seemed to be quite out of kilter.

"Shall I see you back to the house?" His concern was not out of politeness. She could see the genuineness of it written in his furrowed brow and how he came to her directly. "A cup of tea might be just the thing." He took her elbow and turned her toward the house. "And a cake," he whispered, causing her to giggle.

She allowed him to wrap her arm around his and cover her hand where it lay on his arm.

"Your brother and I had a fine ride. We saw two deer near the woods on the far side of the field to the south. One had a fine set of antlers. We might have to go hunting in that area at some point."

Madeline rested her head against his arm. It felt so right to be walking here with him.

"You are quiet," he said a few steps later.

"I am just thinking."

"About what?" His question was soft and filled with care.

Tears, roused by the longing she felt to have him always care for her, pricked her eyes, and her heart raced as the reason for her jealousy became clear as glass.

"I need to speak to my brother."

She had made a horrible decision. She could not allow Fletcher to accept Noah's mysterious friend. She needed Fletcher to convince Noah to consider her, for she wanted him for herself. Oh! But if he was enamoured with this other lady... Her tears could be held back no longer.

"What is it?" Noah stopped walking and wrapped her in his arms.

"There are too many secrets," she managed to say between shuddering breaths.

"Then, let us find Fletcher and put an end to your suffering. I had not wished for that, you know. I would never do anything to harm you."

"I know. I am being foolish." She brushed at her tears with her the palm of her hand when he released her so that they could once again walk toward the house. "I am not normally given to tears you know."

"I am aware of that," he assured her. "I am sorry to be the source of them."

"It is not you." The source of her tears actually was him, of course, but it was not his fault that her heart had finally decided upon what it wanted at the most inopportune time.

They had reached the door to the house, where Fletcher met them.

"What has happened?" He demanded.

"She needs to talk to you," Noah explained. "I do not know more than that." He guided her to the sitting room as it was the closest to the door.

"Some tea, Briggs," Fletcher ordered before pacing just inside the sitting room door while Noah saw her to a seat.

"I will be in the corridor, waiting for my tea," he whispered to her before leaving her to her brother's care.

Fletcher sat down on the sofa next to her.

"You must not accept Noah's friend." There was no need to circumnavigate the issue. It would be best for all concerned if she just came to the point. "I cannot love him."

"What do you mean you cannot love him? You do not even know who he is."

"My heart loves Noah." She hid her face in her hands. "And it cannot because he is in love with someone already."

"But if he is in love with another, then whether you love him or not, you must find someone else to marry."

"I know," she whimpered into her hands.

Fletcher placed a hand on her shoulder and sighed. "I truly think you would like this fellow."

She shook her head. "I cannot. I simply cannot."

"But you know him and have always found him pleasant – well, almost always." He pulled her hands from her face. "Do you trust me?"

"Yes, but I love Noah."

Fletcher pulled out of hsi breast pocket the folded paper on which Noah had written his friend's name and placed it in her hand. "Read it." He stood. "I will be in my study when you wish to yell at me."

"Why would I yell at you?" She turned the note over in her hand.

"Just read it," he said before exiting the room.

Slowly, she unfolded the first fold. Did she really wish to see what was written on this paper? She folded it again and shook her head. What would it change? She loved Noah. Still... her curiosity was aroused. With trembling fingers, she unfolded the note completely. Her breath caught in her chest at what she saw there just as the door opened. There were only two letters, an *m* and an *e*, scratched on that paper.

"It is you?" she asked the gentleman who entered.

Noah nodded. "I needed to know if I had a chance before I put myself forward."

"You?" She looked at those two beautiful letters on the page.

Again, Noah nodded as he knelt before her. "I love you, Maddie. I have for some time."

"Why did you not say something?" She placed a hand on his cheek. He loved her. Her heart wished to burst with joy, and her lips were unable to smile broadly enough to show the extent of her happiness.

"You are Fletcher's little sister. A gentleman just doesn't fall in love with his best friend's sister. It just is not done."

"That is ridiculous." Gentlemen were such strange creatures.

"Perhaps, but if I were to call on you and find that you did not like me, well, I would not just be losing you."

"Wait!" The whole affair started falling into place. "You were talking about me just now when we were in the garden?"

"Yes."

"Oh! So, I have been wishing to hate myself? And feeling guilty for doing so?"

He shrugged and smiled sheepishly.

"And that letter – the one you gave me. Did you send it to yourself?"

He shook his head. "That would be a foolish waste of money."

Her mouth hung open, and she shook her head as he rose from the floor and pulled her to her feet.

"I wrote that letter to you because I wanted you to know how much I admire you." He lifted both of her hands to his lips and kissed them. "Miss Madeline Adcock, will you accept your brother's choice of husband?"

Joy spilled out of her in a laugh. "I did say I would."

"But do you wish to?"

"With all my heart, Noah. With every single bit of my heart."

And with those words, she found herself wrapped in his arms with his lips pressed against hers in the most satisfying and breath-stealing fashion. Her fingers tangled in his hair, holding him to her, satisfying her craving for the caress of his lips, while her body thrilled at the firmness of his against it. And her heart, which had been shrouded for so long in a fog of uncertainty and despair, rejoiced in the light of love that chased away the mist of the past and made way for a gloriously bright and happy future.

Apple Blossoms and Whispering Hearts

Thomas Prescott is awkward and believes himself destined by such to remain a bachelor, but then, he met her. Can he overcome his view of himself to believe that someone as lovely as Clara Watson might actually prefer him to all others?

Chapter 1

"More, Mama! More!"

Thomas Prescott heard the small child's squeal of delight before he rounded the bend in the path and saw her, a small bundle of excitement, dancing with her hands in the air, attempting to catch the white petals falling from the apple tree above.

Thomas stopped where he was. He would eventually have to continue on his way, but he did not wish to disturb the child's fun just yet. He would let her twirl and giggle for a few moments longer before intruding on her play.

"More, Mama!" the child pleaded when the shower of petals slowed.

"One last shake," the lady, who must be the child's mother, said from her perch on a bench beneath the apple tree. "But we must save some flowers so that we can make apple pies for Christmas." Rising up on her toes, she grasped a branch and gave it a gentle shake. The flurry of white petals caused by the action was met with clapping hands, bouncing curls, and happy laughter.

Thomas had always enjoyed watching the exuberance so freely displayed by children. Theirs was a joy that was infectious, though it was also something that felt foreign to him. His childhood had been sober. His mother had died when he was just an infant, and his father had been a dour sort of gentleman who found enjoyment in sedate pursuits and wished for his son to do the same.

If Thomas should ever be blessed with children – which, with each passing year, seemed less and less likely since at forty he still had not found a wife – he would make certain to allow them to run and play as much as they desired until such time as they were required to begin their lessons. However, even then, he would still insist that a portion of their time be spent in pleasurable pursuits merely because they were pleasurable.

He shifted his observation to the petite lady shaking the branch. She must be his new neighbour. He had heard that Mr. and Mrs. Watson had not returned alone but had brought with them a granddaughter and the child's mother, their son's widow. She was pretty just as he had been told. Her hair was the same golden brown as the child's curls and her features were just as delicate.

He should introduce himself instead of just standing like a mesmerized fool on the path. She was his neighbour, not some lady wishing for a dance in an assembly hall. Neighbours were much easier to talk to than strangers – even if he did not know his neighbour, she was a neighbour, just the same.

He drew in a deep breath and willed his feet to carry him forward to complete the task of introductions. These first few steps were always the most difficult. Once these first pleasantries had been exchanged upon this meeting, then it would become easier to touch his hat and nod in greeting or to actually say *good day* whenever they met again.

"Good morning," Mrs. Watson greeted Thomas as he approached.

Smiling, she extended her hand in his direction. "Since you are here, and, even though it is entirely too forward by half to ask such a thing, would you be so kind as to assist me in regaining the ground?"

"I help, Mama." The little girl who was only just head and shoulders above the height of the bench held up her hand towards her mother.

"That is very kind, Abigail," Mrs. Watson said to her daughter. "However, I think it would be far more graceful to allow Mr. –"

"Prescott. Thomas Prescott at your service." Thomas hurried forward to lend his assistance.

"I had thought you might be Mr. Prescott," Mrs. Watson replied before turning back to her daughter. "I should like to have Mr. Prescott assist me. Will you mind terribly, Abigail?"

Abigail scrunched her face as she shook her head. Though she indicated that she did not mind abdicating her position to another, her expression let all know that she was not pleased to be doing so.

"Mr. Pescott?" The child inquired looking up at him with that same scrunched up, not-altogether-pleased expression as he helped her mother from the bench.

While this little lady was far younger than most who raised an eyebrow at something Thomas had done or said, censure from a female was not a foreign thing to him. He was not always at ease in company, and that unease had often led either to some unfortunate, awkwardly-phrased comment or to him being thought aloof and severe because he remained silent. However, unlike disapproval of an older lady, Thomas, who was an uncle to four youngsters, knew precisely how to respond to an unhappy child.

"My humblest thanks, madame, for allowing me the privilege of assisting your mother. It was such a noble act that I believe it deserves some sort of reward." He lifted his walking stick and tapped a branch overhead. Fragrant blossoms fluttered down, and Abigail's scowl dissolved into a happy squeal as she once again attempted to catch the flowers.

As she scampered after petals, Thomas plucked a stem of blossoms from a branch that was within his reach. "For you, Miss — ." He turned to her mother. Although he thought he knew the child's name, he did not wish to presume.

"Watson."

"For you, Miss Watson," Thomas said as he relinquished the flowers to a very pleased Abigail.

"I had heard you were a charmer," Mrs. Watson said with a laugh.

"Me?" Thomas turned to her in surprise.

She nodded.

Thomas shook his head. "You must be mistaken. I am far from charming. In fact, I am quite the opposite."

"Awkward?" Mrs. Watson asked with surprise.

He nodded while she shook her head.

"I cannot believe it," she replied. "You have won over my daughter in mere moments. I dare say anyone who can do that must be charming. Abigail can be very opinionated about who she likes and dislikes."

"Children often are opinionated." Thomas smiled down at the youngster standing next to him. "And often their opinions should be considered carefully, for they have not yet formed the skill of hiding their meaning."

"Which is precisely why you must be as charming as Mother Watson has told me."

Thomas shook his head but protested no further. The way Mrs. Watson's eyes sparkled with approval of him was not something he really wished to argue away. It was excessively pleasant to be approved of by someone as lovely as Mrs. Watson. She might not be in the first blooms of youth, but to him, it did not appear as if any of her beauty had faded.

"I was on my way to call on Mr. and Mrs. Watson as I wished to welcome them to the neighbourhood," Thomas said.

"Then, might we return to the house together?"

"I... I... I do not see why we could not," he replied, somewhat startled by her suggestion. He had thought to ask her if she and Abigail might wish to walk with him, but he had been uncertain if that would be too forward on his part. However, just as she had called to him to assist her when he had thought to offer but had hesitated, she was once again seemingly able to put his thoughts into words on his behalf.

"Might I escort you and your mother home?" he asked Abigail.

The child's face only scrunched for a moment before her head bobbed up and down. "Cake?" she asked, turning wide eyes to her mother.

"Yes, we shall have cake," Mrs. Watson replied. "Now off with you, but do not run too far ahead. I wish to see you to keep you safe."

Abigail scampered up the path as Mrs. Watson accepted Thomas's proffered arm.

"She adores cake," Mrs. Watson whispered.

"She is not alone," Thomas replied.

"Indeed, she is not!" Mrs. Watson agreed with a laugh. "I am certain you already know who I am, but since I was too flustered about not wishing to make a scene by jumping from the bench when we met, I must introduce myself properly now. I am Clara Watson, referred to by many as the Widow Watson, which is a horrible moniker. I prefer simply to be called Clara, but since that is not considered proper by most, Mrs. Clara will suffice to relieve the confusion about whether you are speaking to my mother-in-law or to me."

"It is a pleasure to meet you, Mrs. Clara." He heard her sigh beside him and reframed his words. "It is a pleasure to meet you, Clara."

"Much better, Mr. Prescott," she replied with a smile.

"Thomas," he said. "If I am to be so informal with you, it seems only right that you are equally as informal with me."

"Very well. I shall call you Thomas when we meet like this, but we both know formality will be required of us in company."

She was doing it again, putting words to his

thoughts and making him feel most at ease. She was remarkable, simply and utterly remarkable. Never, in all of his life, had meeting anyone, but most especially a lady, been so very enjoyable.

"I do hope we meet often," he said most sincerely.

Chapter 2

Over the next fortnight, Thomas and Clara did meet often – in the Watson's drawing room, on the street in front of one shop or another, at church as the parishioners exited the building, and, of course, in the orchard among the apple blossoms.

That was perhaps Thomas's favourite place to meet Clara. For in the orchard, there were no prying eyes. There was only the sunshine, the breeze, the trees, and one rather demanding little lady to interfere with their conversation or to cause Thomas to feel any amount of nervousness.

Today, hoping that perhaps he might chance upon Clara and her daughter, he had stopped in the orchard on his walk from Braeburn Grove to Codlin Park. However, he did not happen upon them. Not a giggle was to be heard. Not a beautiful smile was to be seen. He had known he was not likely to find them here. The Watson ladies took their constitutional early in the day for, according to Clara, her daughter was much more inclined to perform as a proper young lady should if some of her wiggles had found their release in the open air along a path that was excessively long for such little legs. Even though he had known Clara and Abigail would likely not be in the orchard, disappointment still settled into his heart as he continued on his way, feeling quite alone.

The barrenness of the orchard hurried his footsteps. If he were fortunate, he would get to present his gift to Abigail before she was taken to the nursery to play while the adults at Codlin Park welcomed callers in the drawing room or found occupation in some sedate task.

As fortune would have it, young Miss Abigail Watson was just being collected by her nursemaid when Thomas entered the drawing room.

"Mr. Pescott."

Thomas pulled his eyes away from the gentleman who sat next to Clara and turned his attention to the little lady in front of him.

"Good day, Miss Watson." The greeting earned him a delighted smile and an attempted good day in return, although it sounded very little like *good day* at all. "Have you had a pleasant morning?"

Abigail's head bobbed up and down. "Pity fowers?" She asked, looking at what he held in his hand.

Thomas crouched down. "For you, Miss Watson." He extended the small stem of apple blossoms to her. "A little something to share with your nurse." He peeked up at the maid who stood behind Abigail and smiled. "I am glad we were able to see each other," he continued speaking to Abigail. "However, I do not wish to keep you from your fun." He rose, bowed, and said, "until tomorrow."

"Curtsy," Abigail's maid whispered, and her young charge immediately performed a rather awkward, yet excessively wonderful, curtsy before leaving the room with one hand in the hand of her nurse and the other clutching tightly to her stem of flowers.

Thomas had wished to bring Clara some flowers as well, but his sister had assured him that doing so was not the thing to do and that it would be much better to present the child with the blossoms. For, according to his sister, the surest way to capture a mother's heart was through her children, and his sister would know since she had four children on whom she doted nearly as much as their uncle did.

From the soft smile Clara wore, it appeared his sister was correct.

"You will spoil her completely," Clara chided, though it did not appear she cared one jot whether he spoiled her daughter with gifts of flowers.

The comment, however, did have the effect of causing Thomas's ears to warm. "My sister accuses me of the same thing about her children."

"The Henry children are far from spoiled," Mr. Spears said. "Have you met them?" he asked Clara, causing Thomas to bristle somewhat.

Clara glanced between the gentleman on her right and Thomas who had taken a seat nearer Mr. Watson. "No," she said, "no, I have not. There are so many whom I have yet to meet."

She looked once again in Thomas's direction. Her eyes seemed to question him. About what, he was not certain. Though perhaps it was his choice of seat.

"I have, however, heard delightful tales about them," she added. "I would say they have a very doting uncle."

"I will not deny that." Thomas smiled at her, and the question in her eye faded somewhat.

"There is an assembly soon," said Mrs. Watson. "Will your sister and her husband attend?"

Thomas nodded. "I would assume so. Margaret is very fond of dancing, and James is hard-pressed not to indulge her."

Mrs. Watson, a small woman with skin that crinkled when she smiled and hair that was half its former shade of brown and half grey, turned her attention to her daughter-in-law. "That will be the best time for you to meet a great number of our neighbours who are more distant."

"An assembly?" Clara questioned as if uncertain that such a thing was a good idea.

"It will be two years next month," Mr. Watson said softly. "I think it is time."

Clara drew and released a small breath. "You are likely correct."

Her eyes dropped to study her hands. It was the first time since meeting her that Thomas had seen Mrs. Clara Watson look anything less than assured of herself.

"I am certain both Mr. Spears and Mr. Prescott would dance a set with you," Mrs. Watson said.

"Mabel," Mr. Watson chided softly. "These gentlemen do not need to be placed in such a situation."

His wife covered her mouth with her fingers and looked from one gentleman to the other. "I do apologize. It is just that I adore Clara and expect others to as well, and if she had a friend or two whom she knew would stand up with her, it might ease her entry into society here a tad."

There was no denying the affection Mrs. Watson claimed to have for her daughter-in-law. It shone in the soft look she was giving Clara.

"It would be no hardship," Thomas said. Securing a set with Abigail now meant that he would have at least one set where he would not have to stand and watch while attempting to arrange his words in his mind before presenting himself to some young lady who would be polite and dance with him but would have eyes for a younger man. He could not blame them. At forty, he was nearly old enough to be the father of most of the young ladies, since there were few single ladies above the age of twenty.

"Oh, none at all," Mr. Spears agreed.

Thomas sighed. Watching Clara dance with

others would make the task of attending the assembly more difficult for he found his heart was very reluctant to share his friend with anyone. However, he was not so selfish as to wish that Clara would have no one else with whom to dance, and he knew that Mr. Spears would be an excellent and kind partner.

Mr. Spears was one of the younger gentlemen who was sought after by many a hopeful miss. He had only just turned thirty and possessed an easy, charming manner. He smiled, and the young ladies sighed. Mr. Spear was just the sort of gentleman which Thomas wished himself to be, for, in addition to his pleasant features and happy disposition, Mr. Spears was all that was honorable.

Put plainly, if Thomas had a daughter of marriageable age, he would welcome Mr. Spears as her suitor. As it was, however, he did not welcome Mr. Spears to be sitting next to Clara in this drawing room, though he likely should. Clara was still young, and in that way, as well as in disposition, she and Mr. Spears seemed an ideal pair.

His heart clenched as he realized what must be done.

Chapter 3

"Oh, Mr. Prescott!"

Thomas stopped his escape and turned toward
Mrs. Watson, who waved to him. He has seen both
her and Clara in Sterling and Sons, but he had
hoped that he could duck into the Grey Hen
before either of them saw him.

"We have not seen you in a week," Mrs. Watson
chided as she approached.

"I do apologize. There has been business needing my attention," he prevaricated.

There had indeed been business matters to be
seen to, but most of them had been things which
were not of a pressing nature. They were reasons
he had given himself for not calling on Clara, tasks
explicitly designed to keep him at home in his
study, on horseback in various parts of his estate,
or in town, as he was today, running triflingly small

errands which could have been completed by someone else. In short, his business for the past week had been to keep himself occupied so that he would not feel the pangs of disappointment that accompanied giving up a lady one admired as he did Clara.

"I hope you have not been left without friends." He looked at Clara, searching for any sign that she might be happy with whoever had taken his place in the Watson's drawing room. Unfortunately, he could not decipher anything from her expression or carriage. But then, he had never been any good at discerning such things.

"We have not been without callers," Clara said. "However, not one of them has brought Abigail any flowers, and she is not pleased."

Distancing himself from Clara was painful enough, but the thought that he was also causing Abigail some distress pierced Thomas's heart. However, this was for the best, he reminded himself. Clara deserved a young, charming husband – not an older, awkward gentleman such as he.

"Mr. Spears is not so charming as you are," Clara added.

His brows furrowed. Could she tell what he was

thinking? She seemed to have an uncanny ability to say things just after he had thought them.

"Oh, not at all," Mrs. Watson hurried to assure him. "Do not get me wrong, he is a lovely man. However, there has most certainly been something missing from our lives this past week, and I will not countenance it any longer. There are only so many times a grandmother can see her granddaughter looking out the window and repeating your name before that grandmother must take matters into her own hands." She gave Thomas a stern look. "You will find an invitation to dinner when you return home. It is for tomorrow evening. I will not accept any reply other than you intend to join us."

"But I was going to see my man of business late tomorrow afternoon." It was not a lie. He had intended to check on some things. Of course, none of those things were urgent matters.

"That is unfortunate," Clara said softly, her lips tipping into a quick small, sad smile when he glanced her direction. Did she miss him, or was she just disappointed on her daughter's behalf?

"I am certain we could shift our meeting," he said before he could think better of it. Attending a dinner was not the best way to give his place to Mr. Spears.

"We would not wish to inconvenience you," Clara assured him.

"You are not."

"Excellent!" Mrs. Watson declared. "Then, when Abigail stands at the window today and asks for you, I can tell her that she will see you tomorrow."

Thomas shifted his weight from his left foot to his right and looked down at the ground. "I do apologize. I did not think my business would cause any unhappiness for Miss Watson." If he were abjectly honest, he would have to admit that he had only considered his own unhappiness from being separated from both Abigail and her mother.

Mrs. Watson grasped Thomas's forearm. "She is not the only one who has missed you," she said with a wink and a tip of her head toward Clara.

Part of Thomas's heart rejoiced that he had been missed, while another part of it ached, and he once again wondered if he was doing the best thing by allowing Clara the opportunity to get to know Mr. Spear without his presence to divide her attention. How many nights had he lain awake wondering if it was not best to just continue as friends and let Clara's choices take a more natural path away from him and toward Mr. Spear?

"I cannot say I have not missed calling," he admitted. How many times had he found his feet taking him in the direction of the Watson's orchard, only to turn himself around with a heavy heart?

"Then a dinner is just the thing that everyone has needed," Mrs. Watson said.

"I believe you are correct," Thomas assured Mrs. Watson, though he was not entirely certain she was. "Until tomorrow." He tipped his hat and took his leave.

~*~*~

Thomas tossed the things he had purchased on the seat of his gig and climbed up next to them. As much as he wished for a good, stout pint at the Grey Hen, he thought it would likely not give him the advice he needed. Therefore, he turned his vehicle toward his sister's house.

Eight dusty miles later, he found himself at his sister Margaret's door.

"Thomas!" she cried in delight when he entered

the drawing room. "This is a surprise. What brings you to visit me?"

She gave him a hug and a kiss on his cheek. There were only two years that separated them in age, and though he was oldest, he found his younger sister was often the one to whom he could turn for advice. She seemed to understand him like no other.

"Why did you marry James?" he asked, jumping feet first into what he needed to know.

"Because I love him, of course," she answered with a laugh. "Which you already know because it was you who gave me permission to marry him after gaining a very clear assurance that I loved him and was not just taking the first offer to come my way."

Thomas shook his head. "I asked that badly. Of course, I know how you feel about your husband. It is not something one has to ask about to find an answer. One has only to see the two of you together to know that your marriage is founded on love."

"Well, then, dear brother, perhaps you could clarify what it is that you wish to know. Tea?" She rang the bell before he could reply that a cup would be lovely.

Thomas took another stab at inquiring after the information he needed. "Why do you love James?" He scowled. That was nearly the correct wording, but not quite.

"What I mean is, what made you love him? He has a fine home to be sure, and an outstanding living, but – and I apologize for offending – he is not handsome in the classical sense. He is tall and broad, which, it seems, many appreciate, but his features are plain. Not that he is deficient." He felt like he was stammering as he attempted to explain himself. "But he is nothing out of the ordinary."

"Much like you?" Margaret asked.

"Yes." That was the heart of the matter.

She shrugged. "I am not certain I can say. My heart chose him. Even when I first met him, I felt as if I was in the presence of a dear, trusted friend. I longed to spend every moment with him. To share all my joys and sorrows. I never once feared he would reject me for my looks or being foolish or – well, anything, really." She smiled and sighed. "And, when he took my hand for that first dance, an attraction to more than his presence danced up my arm and lodged itself in my heart. I knew I could never desire another as I desired him. It matters not what he looks like now or what he will look like in thirteen years from now when our daughters are on the cusp of being presented to society. I love him for who he is, and I always will."

"You would not have chosen another who was more charming?"

"I found no other to be as charming as James."

"No one?" Thomas asked incredulously as Clara's words about Mr. Spear not being as charming as he resounded in his mind.

His sister shook her head. "Once my heart had made its choice, there was no turning aside."

He walked to the window and stared out at the drive for a full five minutes as he pondered that thought. Could it be that Clara's heart had chosen him? He turned toward his sister and opened his mouth to speak but waited until a tray, containing a few biscuits alongside a teapot and cups, was placed on the table at the far end of the room.

Silently, he follows his sister to the table. She gave him a curious look but said not a word. She had rarely ever pressed him for information, for pressing him on a matter only resulted in sharp words and his thoughts being more muddled than they had started out being. Instead, she would wait until he was ready to speak. Just as she was doing now.

"Do you think it is possible for a heart to make such a choice twice in one lifetime?"

He took a seat as she lifted the teapot's lid and peeked inside. He knew she looking to see if the tea was as dark as she liked it. A weak cup of tea was not something to be borne where his sister was concerned.

"Is this about Mrs. Clara Watson?" She sat and offered him a biscuit.

He nodded. They had sat around this very table discussing Thomas's charming new neighbour not so very long ago. Back when he had been hopeful that there might be a match to be made. Back before he had considered Mr. Spear.

"I have been attempting to distance myself from her."

"You have what?" Margaret cried. "Oh, no! You have not!"

"I have," Thomas replied with a shrug. "Clara is young. She deserves someone closer in age to her. Mr. Spear –"

"Do not tell me you are attempting to match her with another?"

It was as he had feared. His plan was flawed, although he was not exactly sure why.

"I am nearly forty – almost ten years older than Mr. Spear, and Clara is not yet thirty."

"And James is ten years my senior," Margaret argued.

"Ten years is not as many as thirteen or fourteen," Thomas protested.

Margaret pursed her lips and shook her head. "Age has very little to do with anything, Thomas."

"But she has been widowed once already." His voice was barely above a whisper, and he ran a finger along the edge of the table in front of him.

His sister sat down, teapot still in her hand, the cups she had been filling forgotten. "And was Mr. Watson ancient?"

Thomas lifted startled eyes to her. "Not to my knowledge."

"Death is not a respecter of age, Thomas."

"But it is more likely as we grow older."

"I will not refute that." She smiled at him as tears glistened in her eyes. "You love her so much?"

"I care for her very much," Thomas said with a nod of his head.

"Enough to not wish for her to grieve over losing you."

"Yes."

"And so, you attempt to arrange for this loss now rather than later?"

Thomas's eyes grew wide as the reason why his plan was flawed finally dawned on him.

Margaret reached across the table toward him, and he responded by grasping her hand. "Go to her, Thomas. Let her choose."

Something very like peace, though slightly less settled, washed over him. He had known his sister would be able to help him sort out what was right, even if her advice was daunting. No lady had ever chosen Thomas. But, perhaps, that was not to be the result this time. Perhaps.

"I am dining with the Watsons tomorrow." He accepted the cup of tea his sister had finally finished pouring for him.

"Good." She placed the teapot back on the tray and gave him a stern look before taking up her own cup. "And then call on her."

"I will." Thomas did not think he had ever made such a more sure promise in his life.

"Now," Margaret said, settling into her chair, "tell me all about her and her little girl."

Happily, Thomas obliged.

Chapter 4

Thomas pulled out his pocket watch and checked the time. Three minutes. His horse should be saddled and ready by now.

He made one last note for his steward and then rose from his desk. All was ready for their meeting which had been moved from today until tomorrow.

Leaving his study, he hurried to the grand staircase and took the steps two at a time.

"Is everything well sir?" His butler called to him.

"Yes, yes. All is well," Thomas called back. "I just do not wish to be late."

His nerves had been in a state of heightened animation ever since yesterday when he left his sister's home with a new plan in place. There was no way – absolutely none – for him to be sedate when the happiness of his future seemed so near to being decided.

Entering his room, he made quick work of washing his hands and changing his shirt, jacket, and cravat. Then, with his gift for Abigail in his hand, he dashed down the stairs, collected his hat from his slightly amused looking butler, and exited his house.

His horse was waiting as he had expected, and after a quick look at his watch, he swung up onto the beast, retrieved his parcel from the groom to whom he had given it so he could mount, and was off. With any luck, he would be on time.

He breathed a sigh of relief when he rounded the corner in the path, which led through the orchard, and saw that he was not too late.

Clara was sitting on the bench under the apple tree while Abigail was crouched down close to the ground examining something of interest to a child of two and which would likely be overlooked by anyone above the age of ten. That is, she was crouched down until she heard his horse. Then, Abigail stood and, turning toward the sound, clapped her hands and bounced with delight.

"Mr. Pescott! Mr. Pescott!" she cried.

"Miss Watson," he greeted.

Clara rose from the bench. "May I help you with that?" She pointed to the pot he held.

Did she always know what he was thinking before he spoke? He smiled. She was a lot like his sister in that way.

"Yes, if you could take this, it would make dismounting much easier."

"What is it?" Abigail asked.

"It is a present," Thomas replied as he gained the ground.

"Present?" The child's eyes were wide with curiosity.

"For a special young lady," he said.

"Me?"

Thomas laughed. "Yes, Miss Watson, this gift is for you, but you must promise me that you will care for it well. There is to be no poking fingers into the dirt or dumping it out."

Her brow furrowed, and her lips pursed as she bobbed her head up and down.

He took the pot from her mother, and crouching down, he asked, "Do you see these little green shoots? Touch them gently," he added when she put out a hand toward the pot. "Those are baby flowers."

"Pity flowers?"

"Yes, they will be very pretty flowers when they grow bigger. My sister is an excellent gardener, and she allowed me to have this plant to give to you." He held the pot out to her.

"Pity flowers." She looked up to her mother with a smile.

"Shall I keep the pot for you, Abigail, so that you can play some more?"

Abigail placed her chubby little hands on Thomas's gloved ones and moved the pot in her mother's direction.

Clara took it and placed it on the bench. "What do you tell Mr. Prescott?"

Little arms wound around Thomas's neck as Abigail muttered a thank you. Thomas hugged her briefly in return, and then, took her hand so she could show him the ants she had been watching. Then, once she was satisfied that he had seen them long enough, he was allowed to join her mother on the bench under the apple tree.

"The blossoms are almost gone," he said as he sat down.

"They are."

"My sister thought that the potted plant would

be a welcome diversion, and I agreed. I hope you do not mind."

He had longed for this moment to be alone with her in the orchard since he had set his plan in his mind yesterday. However, now that it was here, he was fearful. No lady had ever chosen him before.

"I am delighted that both you and your sister thought of Abigail."

He studied Clara's face. It seemed, from her smile, that she was truly delighted.

"I have missed sitting here," he admitted.

"I have missed having you here," she replied.

"I have been contemplating something." He shifted nervously, and she placed a reassuring hand on his arm, which he covered quickly so that she would not remove it. "Perhaps it was foolish to even consider it, but..." He squeezed her hand and looked up at the branches of the tree across from them. It would be quite nice if the words he had rehearsed would grace him with their presence in his mind, but it seemed that such was not to be.

"Yes," she whispered.

He turned questioning eyes to her.

"If you were wondering if I would consider you

as a suitor or if you were wondering if I preferred you to Mr. Spear, the answer is yes," she clarified.

His lips tipped up into a half-smile. "How do you always know what I am thinking?"

She shrugged. "I do not know. There is just something about you that speaks to me."

He blew out a breath. "There is something about you that calls to me."

She smiled. "And what does this something say?"

He turned and took both of her hands in his. "It says to make you mine. To pursue you until you agree to be my wife. That there is no one any-where in this world who would complete me as you would."

Her head dipped, and her cheeks grew rosy. "And do you believe this something?"

"You mean does it speak the truth?"

She nodded. "Does it?"

"Very much so," he answered. "However, there is something in me that worries that I am not what or who you need. I am not young. I am clumsy with my words, and I do not always know what the best thing is to do when it comes to ladies. There are many who are –"

"Not you," she inserted, completing his thought but not as he had intended for it to be completed. "There are also a great number of people who are not me."

His brow furrowed. He was uncertain what she meant.

She took one of her hands from him and placed it on his cheek. "Of all the places in the world and of all the people in the world, it was chosen that I should be here with you. The path to this spot was not easy, but if you would have me, the journey would be worth the prize."

She took her other hand from him and placed it on his other cheek so that his face was framed by her hands. "I never thought to love again, Thomas. I thought my opportunity for such had been brief and was gone. But it is not."

"It is not?"

She shook her head.

"You would choose me over Mr. Spear?"

"I would choose you over anyone."

"That is quite remarkable," he said as a smile spread across his face and joy bubbled over in his heart. No lady had ever chosen him before. "You would marry me if I were to ask?"

She nodded as she began to remove her hands from his face. Without a thought, he took them and drew her to her feet.

"Will you marry me, Clara?" He could feel his expression mirroring the happiness he saw in hers.

"Yes, if you will say that you will love me — and Abigail — for always."

"Always," he assured her. "My heart would not let me do any less." He wanted to pull her into his embrace and seal their agreement with a kiss, but he hesitated, still just the smallest bit unsure of himself.

"Kiss me, Thomas."

"How do you always know what I am thinking?" he asked.

Clara laughed. "Oh, Thomas, there is just something about you that speaks to me, and I rather think it is your heart which communes with mine because I love you."

And with those words echoing in his heart and mind, Thomas wrapped his arms around her and pressed his lips to hers, kissing her for the first of many, many times here under the apple tree while apple blossoms floated down from the branches above and a small bundle of excitement clapped her hands and danced nearby.

A Lily in Midwinter

A misdirected letter sets a scheme in motion which, when it draws to its conclusion, should see Frederick George happily trapped. However, if he discovers the scheming, the outcome might be as bleak as a midwinter's day.

Chapter 1

And so it begins. We must leave in a fortnight, and Mother has had the modiste to the house twice just this week to alter my gowns. There was no need for it. They fit just fine. However, she is convinced that a few more embellishments or a little less room to breath will help them make me more desirable to some quizzing glass-carrying fop.

Frederick Bartholomew George looked at the directions on the front of the rain dampened letter a second time. Those smudges definitely looked as if they were his address, but the letter was most certainly not meant for him. According to the address on the front, it was meant for an *S. G– something.* Rain and ink were not friends. What one attempted to make clear, the other washed away. Perhaps there was a name in the letter which would give some indication as to for whom this letter was intended.

That is not fair of me to count all gentlemen as pea-cocks, but you know how it is. Mama has her ideas about what constitutes an acceptable husband, which, you know full well, are not the same as mine.

Oh, Sally, I am torn. I want so much to see you, but I dread our visit to your home for it will mark the end of a pleasant autumn of books and unchaperoned walks and the beginning of a trying season filled with 'stand tall', 'smile', 'my is he not the most handsome gentleman you have ever seen', and the like.

Please write and assure me that all will be well, and that I will be able to weather the machinations of my mother long enough to find a suitable husband. I have no time to write more, for we must be off at once to secure some ghastly concoction from the milliner. (It will be lovely, I am sure. However, at present, I am very ill-disposed to liking much of anything.)

I send my love to you and yours.

Yours affectionately,

Lily

Sally? He searched his memory for any gently bred young lady he knew who was called Sally. Sadly, he could not think of one. If he knew who she was, he would send this letter to her straight-away. However, all he knew was that he was not Sally, and Miss Lily Whoever-She-Was would not be receiving a letter in reply to calm her nerves about her mother's matchmaking ways. Unless...

He put the letter on his desk and leaned back in his chair. There was a return address. He could inform Miss Lily that her letter had been delivered to the wrong person. Recognizing that this was likely the best idea, he opened his writing box, took out a pen, and uncapped his ink. He drew a line under Miss Lily's closing remarks and began to write.

Dear Miss Lily,

(Forgive me, but there was no surname attached to your signature and the name on the outside of the letter was smudged. I am afraid it has been dreadfully rainy lately, and it is preventing me from being more formal in my address.)

It is my regrettable task to inform you that your letter has not reached its intended destination and has, instead, landed on my desk amongst a pile of papers. I thank you for the diversion your missive has provided, and I wish to express my condolences regarding your mother. I know some of what you face, for I also have a mother, as well as a sister, who are both anxious to see me married. However, I willingly admit that my being a gentleman does put me at somewhat of an advantage, though only marginally, as my mother is a terrific schemer.

I am returning this to you in hopes that your friend will eventually receive your news and that she might send you her assurances.

Sincerely and with best wishes for your impending travels and season,

F.B. George

There. He read Miss Lily's letter once again and chuckled at the seeming disparity between mother and daughter. Then, he reread his own. It was brief and friendly. Not at all stiff and business-like. He had tried to keep it in a tone which he might use if writing to his sister or his good friend. From what he could see, he had succeeded. Confident that there should not be a thing for Miss Lily to find wrong with his note, he sealed it and had it posted before returning to the much less interesting estate matters which still remained on his desk

~*~*~

"I heard Flitcroft instructing a footman to see something sent by express." Frederick's mother kept her eyes on her dinner plate and meticulously cut her venison into tiny pieces while she pried into her son's life.

"A letter was misdirected, and I wished to have it returned as quickly as possible." The roasted celeriac was particularly good this evening, nearly as tasty as the mushrooms in butter sauce. Nearly, but not quite.

"Who was it for?" His younger sister's fork on which was skewered both a slice of venison and a mushroom hung just over her plate as she turned to her attention to her brother.

She was far too curious by half, in his opinion, and his mother did little to curb such behaviour. In fact, his mother was looking just as expectantly at him as his sister was.

"The directions were somewhat spoiled by the rain."

"You could not make them out at all?" She finally popped her bite of food into her mouth. He should be free from questions from her for a minute or two.

He shook his head. "The names were the worse for the wear, I am afraid. The person for whom the letter was intended has the initials S.G. That is all I know other than the sender's name is Lily.

"Lily?" A curious look passed between his mother and sister. "That is a very pretty name, do you not think, Rosalie?"

"Simply lovely. I would imagine the lady who bears such a name to be quite delicate, much like this cup." She lifted her teacup and took a sip.

Why she refused to have wine with her meal, he did not know. But she did. It was always tea with dinner and wine with a bit of something sweet later. It was completely against how things should be done if you asked him.

"See how it is so delicately painted?" She held the cup in his direction. "There is not a garish flower on here. Just simple rosebuds twining around each other in a field of white, bordered by a golden band."

Roses were a favourite in his family, and all the cups and saucers in this particular set of dishes paid homage to his grandmother's favourite flower.

"She did not sound delicate," Frederick muttered, returning to his delightful mushrooms. His sister could be so fanciful.

"What did you say, Freddie?" Rosalie skewered her brother with a pointed look.

"I said that she did not sound delicate," he repeated as he attempted to avoid both his sister's and his mother's raised brows. "I read the letter," he admitted.

"You did what?"

He winced at his mother's sharp tone.

"I know that it is rude to read someone else's correspondence, and yet it was necessary."

It was also rude to read the words written in a journal which was not his, and it was beyond the pale to stand close enough to someone's shoulder so that he could read a letter as it was being written. How many times had his curious nature won him that lecture as a child?

"I was looking to see if I could discover to whom the letter was addressed so that I might find its rightful owner. It was intended for some lady named Sally. That is all I know."

"No, it is not all you know," Rosalie said, her lips were pursed with displeasure when he looked at her. "You said Lily did not sound delicate, and there must be a reason for such disparagement of a lady you do not even know."

"I was not disparaging," he defended.

"You said she was not delicate."

"Exactly." That was not a disparagement. It was a statement of observation. And there was, in his mind, absolutely nothing wrong with being considered *not delicate*. In fact, if he were pushed to be blunt, he'd rather have a lady who was *not delicate*.

"Delicate means easily broken. Miss Lily did not sound easily broken."

She sounded rather as if she might be capable of withstanding a great deal of disagreeableness with just a sardonic word and a roll of her eyes. The thought brought a smile to his lips. He might like to meet this Lily.

"A lady may be delicate *and* strong," his mother cautioned, drawing his mind back to the conversation at hand rather than allowing him to continue imagining Miss Lily. "A teacup holds very hot water without so much as a whimper of complaint. Fine features and manners do not indicate a lack of fortitude."

Frederick sighed, loudly, purposefully, and with a look of exasperation for his mother. "I am certain that is true. Could we please not make this into a lesson on what I should be looking for in a wife?"

His mother batted her lashes and smiled. "Would I do that?"

"Yes. And it would likely come with a list of ladies whom you think I should court."

"You are not getting any younger."

"Thank you, Mother. I had forgotten," he retorted wryly.

She was laughing at him behind her wine goblet. He could tell by the way her eyes were dancing. She did like to tease him about his need to marry.

"Since I am nearly thirty – it is only three years away as you might remember – perhaps I should just propose to the next lady who enters our door."

"I would not be opposed to that." His mother smirked at him as she returned her glass to the table.

That was not the response he had hoped for from his mother. She was supposed to tell him that he was being foolish or some such thing. The eyebrow over his left eye arched.

"Are we expecting guests?"

"It is nearly Christmas," his mother said.

How had he forgotten? His mother always entertained at Christmas. Of course, there would be guests. Their period of mourning was over. The thought was sobering and tinged with sadness.

"A dear friend of mine from my school years is coming to visit. We see each other each year in town during the season – when I am there. At one time, she visited here on a regular basis, but, with how busy life gets as one's children get older, it has been years since she has visited Rose Hall.

"However, her youngest daughter is to take in the season in town this year, and since our estate is closer to London than theirs is and could very well be her last year to be required to take in the season, it seemed a good plan to have her visit on her way." She took a sip from her wine glass. "Her husband will join us, but not until she and her daughter have been here for a fortnight."

"Will it not be fabulously grand to have so many around our table for the Christmas feast this year?" His sister was far too excited.

"I take it you know who these people are?"

Rosalie's head bobbed up and down. "I have met the daughter, and we get on famously."

"But this is the daughter's first time in town for the season, is it not? How have you met her?"

"One can be in town for reasons other than the season."

He scowled at her. That was not a very good explanation.

"Her older sister just married this past June," Rosalie said. "Now, it is her turn. She has been in town but not part of the season proper on account of her sister."

He nodded. That made sense. It was not unusual for only one daughter to be presented at a time in order to put her at as good an advantage as possible in securing a husband.

"Do these people have a name?" He should likely know who would be arriving at his house. His mother was usually good about informing him of these details, and that she had not was excessively suspicious.

"Of course, they do, silly," his sister replied before taking up her teacup once again and deigning to not tell him anything further.

He looked to his mother. "Would someone please share this tidbit of information with me? I should like to know who I will be hosting."

"Do you really need to know it?" Rosalie asked.

"Yes." Why would he not need to know the name of his guests?

"The family name is Brinson," his mother answered, causing Rosalie to roll her eyes as if displeased that such information had been shared.

"And it is just Mrs. Brinson, Miss Brinson, and eventually Mr. Brinson who will be spending the yuletide with us?"

"Yes." His mother sighed. "Your father enjoyed having guests."

Frederick settled back into his chair. He wished his father was still here to see to all the guests and festivities at Rose Hall. However, he was not and had not been for what would be two years come spring. Frederick was not as at ease with guests as his father had been. He was more likely than not to inadvertently cause offense.

"I will do my best," he assured his mother.

She smiled. "I know you will. Just be yourself, and they will have to love you."

He doubted that. His mother had a far rosier opinion of him than most did. To her, he could do very little wrong – other than refusing to consider marrying one of her many suggestions, that is.

"I agree." Rosalie was smiling as if she knew a

secret. "And you must believe me because I barely tolerate you many days." She batted her lashes.

He chuckled. "I should hate to see how cossetted I would be if you found me more than tolerable." This, as expected, drew a laugh from both his mother and sister. They were two ladies cut from the same clothe. Two very lovely ladies.

"Wait. You are not attempting to match me with Miss Brinson, are you?"

"No!" they both replied almost too quickly. He would have to be on his guard.

"Did we not promise we would not meddle after that fiasco two years ago? I truly did not know Miss White was such a harridan, or I would not have pushed her at you," his mother said.

His mother had been terrifically apologetic when it came to light that the lady she was championing as the best choice of the season had a foul temper and razor-sharp tongue which she used to slice apart anyone who did not do as she thought they should. The lady hid it well enough in public, unless she thought that her prize, which happened to be him at the time, was being snatched from her.

"Yes, you did promise," he agreed, "but I know how you both are."

"It would not be so bad if you were to like Miss Brinson," Rosalie admitted. "Not that I am suggesting you should. I am only assuring you that if you do, I will not feel as if you are attempting to steal my friend from me, and I can assure you that she is in no way a harridan."

"I will keep that in mind." They might say they were not meddling, but he was nearly positive they were. But what could be done, save to be vigilant?

He looked from one to the other of the ladies he held dear. "Very well, I shall pretend to believe you." He rose from his chair.

"Are you not going to stay for dessert?" his mother asked. "It is carrot cake."

Frederick paused at the door. Carrot cake was on his list of favourite sweet indulgences. "Perhaps you could send a piece to me in my study?"

"Are you going to hide from us all evening?" his sister asked. "I had hoped to play a game or two."

He smiled at his sister. "If I can have carrot cake while adding that final column of numbers and a glass of Madeira when I join you, then I shall play whatever you wish." He held up a finger. "As long as the game does not end with me being married."

"I have no idea what you have against marrying," she called after him.

He had nothing against the institution of marriage. He just needed to find the right lady, and that, to this point in his life, remained the sticking point.

Chapter 2

"Begging your pardon," a maid carrying a basket of brushes and clothes scooted by Frederick as he was making his way to his study after returning from a morning ride.

The house had been a flurry of activity for a week and a half now. Everything must be cleaned and polished before their guests arrived. It did not matter to his mother than not all the rooms would be in use. Indeed, several would be shut up to conserve on fuel. However, if either Miss Brinson or her mother were to wander into the wrong room, his mother would be absolutely mortified for them to find a speck of dust on a tabletop or a spent candle in a holder.

The smell of soap and the sound of sneezes hung about the place during the day. Two more days of the servants industriously attending to their duties, and all would be ready.

"I am thinking partridge pie would be nice for dinner," his mother popped her head into his study. "Were you successful this morning?"

"I did not go shooting, Mother. The gamekeeper will have to assist you with your desire for partridge today."

He stirred the coals in the grate, thankful that a fire awaited him. The day was not warm. The air was damp enough to chill a person to the bone, though no rain fell. With the wind as frigid as it was, Frederick expected that snow would fall from the grey sky instead of rain. It was December, after all, and snow as just as likely as rain.

"I did see a couple of nice plump birds, however."

"That is not going to do me any good," his mother scolded. She drew and released a deep breath. "I suppose I shall have to send word to Mr. Morris before speaking to Cook."

"That would seem the best plan." He bit back a smile when she scowled. She had likely hoped he would send a message to Mr. Morris. "Send a footman to me, and I will send him on his way to Mr.

Morris. You know he only seems grumbly. He is actually a rather agreeable chap."

"Maybe to you. I think he does not like ladies."

"That might explain why he has never married," Frederick quipped. "I think it was his mother who put him off the notion." He settled into the chair behind his desk and gave his mother a pointed look before smiling at her. "Seriously, he does not speak well of her. I am sorry to say that I do not think she liked children."

"Children can be trying," his mother teased.

"Send a footman," Frederick said before she ducked out of his study.

While he waited, he picked up the stack of correspondence he had dropped on his desk yesterday. One envelope caught his eye as he shuffled through the letters. It bore his name and was written in an elegant, feminine sort of style. He smiled as he read the address of the sender, noting that no name was included with that bit of information.

Eagerly, he broke the seal to see what Miss Lily had to say. No doubt, she wished to thank him for returning her misdirected letter.

A loud thump followed by a raised voice in the adjoining room filtered through the door that room shared with his study. No doubt some unfortunate maid had knocked over something and was being scolded.

"You wished to see me?" A footman stood nervously at his door.

"My mother would like to have partridge pie for dinner. Could you please see that Mr. Morris knows to supply the needed bird to the kitchen before too late in the day?"

"Yes, sir. Was there anything else?"

"No, you may be on your way. Would you close the door, please?"

The young man did as requested, and Frederick turned his attention to the tantalizing piece of paper he held in his hand.

Mr. George,

It is not proper, sir, for one to read letters addressed to persons who are not they.

"Yes, my mother has told me many times," he muttered at the missive.

You should have known as soon as you began reading it that the letter in your possession was not for you. While it is not at all acceptable for you to know about my struggles with my mother,

Miss Lily was not delicate by any stretch of the

imagination, and yet, though she was scolding him, he did not mind. She was not saying anything that was not truthful, even if she was saying it bluntly. This was the sort of lady he preferred to the simpering ones he had met in town. Any one of them would never have had the audacity to chide a stranger – especially an unmarried gentleman stranger.

I am grateful that you have informed me of the error which was made in delivery. I have sent a new letter to my friend. I am certain she will be delighted to receive it.

There was the pretty rose pattern. He smiled. Perhaps she was a teacup, a good stout one with a sturdy handle.

Regards,

Miss Lily (It is best if you do not know my full name as correspondence between an unmarried gentleman and a lady could be viewed as scandalous.)

Frederick chuckled. The impertinent Miss Lily was worried about being scandalous, was she?

He opened his writing supplies and dipped his pen in ink.

Miss Lily,

Thank you for reminding me of what my mother has always taught me. I should not have read the letter had it not been necessary to do so in an attempt to discover if I could be of service in helping it reach the intendent party. I profusely apologize.

With my sincerest wishes for your good health and a tolerable season,

F.B. George (*You will note that I have returned to you both letters which you have sent to me so that there can be no concern that I should use your correspondence to ensnare a wife. I do hope you will be as noble and burn both missives after you have received this one.*)

He bit his thumbnail as he reread the note he had scrawled out. It was likely too teasing. He was not known to tease strangers, and while, for some reason, Miss Lily did not seem all that much like a stranger, she was indeed a stranger. He put his pen away and set the letter to the side. He would give whether or not to post it more consideration later.

However, later was not so far away as he had thought it would be, for the very next letter he withdrew from his correspondence was from Miss Lily. There was no name in the return address, but he was becoming familiar with her directions and her penmanship. He turned the letter over in his hand as he contemplated breaking the seal and reading what she had written to her friend. He shook his head. Why had she sent this letter to the same mistaken address? He flipped the letter over again.

S. George? His left eyebrow cocked. The direction and the surname fit his residence. It was only that S which did not. He sat back in his chair and pondered that fact for a full two minutes before going in search of his sister. Perhaps she would know a Sally George.

~*~*~

"Are you certain you do not know a Sally George?" he asked his sister for a third time. She was avoiding looking at him. He was almost certain she knew something she was not sharing.

She nodded — weakly if you asked him.

"Well, then, I suppose I shall have to return this to Miss Lily and inform her that whomever this Sally George is, she is playing a devious trick on her and is likely not the sort of friend a lady should keep."

"You cannot!" Rosalie cried. "Why, Lily is on her way to visit her friend."

He had started to rise from the ivory sofa on which they sat, but on hearing her words, he dropped back down onto the piece of furniture. "How do you know that?"

"Know what?" she asked sweetly.

"How do you know that she is on her way to visit a friend?"

"You mentioned it at dinner that night."

Her cheeks were growing rosy.

"No, I did not. Try again."

With a huff, she took the letter from his hand. "I am Sally."

Frederick blinked.

"Rosalie – Sally," she said as she broke the seal to the letter she held.

He covered her hands with his. "Why did you not tell me at dinner?"

She shrugged.

His brow furrowed. "And your being Sally does not explain how you knew what was in a letter that arrived sealed on my desk."

She grimaced. "I know how to seal a letter."

His mouth dropped open as what she had done became clear to him. "You read the letter, resealed it, and placed it with my mail?"

She nodded.

"Why?" He shook his head. "No, do not tell me.

This is some attempt to match me with your friend." His heart dropped into his stomach. "Miss Brinson."

Again, his sister grimaced. "Lily is a sweet girl. She would make a wonderful sister."

He scrubbed his face with his hands. "Does Miss Brinson know that you are trying to match her with your brother?" The upcoming visit could be exceptionally uncomfortable rather than just holding the normal amount of discomfort. "She is likely having a good chuckle at my expense."

"She would not. I have not told her that I would like her to marry you, though I have spoken very highly of you to her."

"How can she not be laughing at me. Surely, she must know that the Mr. George who sent her a letter is your brother." He rubbed the back of his neck. "And how am I to greet her with any sort of dignity? You know I stumble over such things as it is."

Rosalie but a hand on his arm. "She does not know it is you. She has asked if we have a neighbour with the same name. She thinks it must be a relation. See?"

He took the letter his sister held out to him. "An

ungentlemanly neighbour or a presumptuous relation." He leveled a glare at his sister. "I do not see how that is supposed to make me feel any better about this."

Rosalie sighed. "I thought you might take up a correspondence that would make you more at ease. You are much more relaxed when you write things than when you speak."

That was true. The words flowed from his mind to his quill much more easily than they did to his mouth. It had always been so. It was likely due to the fact that written words could be retracted and consigned to the fire before they were seen.

"She scolded me for having read her letter."

"Lily wrote to you?" There was an unwelcome hint of excitement in his sister's voice.

"She did, and I was about to reply in a rather impertinent fashion. However, I shall see that the letter is burned."

"Oh, send it!" Rosalie cried.

"I cannot. Just imagine how put out she will be if she discovers I knew who she was before I sent it?" He shook his head. "I cannot. She will think I am playing some horrible game at her expense."

"Lily is not stuffy," Rosalie assured him. "She would find it amusing."

While, from her letter, Frederick believed that Miss Brinson was not stuffy – or, at least, not entirely stuffy – he was not convinced that she would find his reply, as he had written it, to be in the least bit amusing. He sighed. "Do I need to worry about her mother? Miss Lily's first letter implied that her mother was the matchmaking sort."

Rosalie pulled her bottom lip between her teeth and winced.

Oh, good heavens! Was it possible for him to spend Christmas in town? He growled and rose from the sofa.

"Mother!" he shouted.

His sister grasped his hand. "She loves you, as do I."

He pulled his hand away from her. "Do you think you could try to not love me so well for just a few weeks?" Tears sprang to her eyes, causing him to immediately regret his words. "I know you mean well," he added before giving her forehead a kiss and crossing the room to bellow for his mother once again.

Chapter 3

Five days later, as Frederick was attempting to read while his mother stitched and his sister alternated between sitting on the settee, flipping through a fashion magazine, and rising to pace to the window so she could peek out at the drive, the near serenity of the familial portrait was disrupted by a squeal of delight.

"What is it?" Frederick looked up from the book he was reading.

"They are here." His sister clapped her hands like a young girl of twelve instead of the relatively mature nineteen-year-old she was.

While excitement filled his younger sister at the prospect of greeting the Brinsons, it created quite the opposite sensation in Frederick. He blew out a breath and reminded himself that he had prepared for this. It had taken four attempts, but finally, last evening, he had arrived at, and written out, what he hoped would be an appropriate greeting for his guests. He glanced at the door which connected this sitting room to his study. Perhaps he should read over what he had written once more to guarantee that he had committed it to memory properly.

"Smiling might be good." His mother face was pinched with concern as she watched him.

"I am not as good at this as Father was." He kept his voice pitched low.

It was perhaps not all of what was causing his hands to sweat and his chest to tighten, but it was part of it. The weight of being the head of the family always settled most firmly upon him when faced with the prospect of filling his father's role. He had come to be at ease with overseeing the estate because he had been doing that on a nearly daily basis for nigh onto two years now. However, greeting guests, who were to stay at his home, had never happened in that time, and that meant that this was the first time he would be the other half of his mother's hospitality and not just her son. He puffed out his cheeks and then expelled the air they contained.

"You have always acquitted yourself very well as a proper young man. You worry too much."

"It is a fault I own." Worrying seemed as natural as breathing to him.

"Just be yourself, my darling. You shall not disappoint me or your father."

He gave her a curt nod. He did not wish to talk about how he longed to be as good a man as his father had been. Such a topic would not make the fluttering in his heart or the small but pronounced thumping in his neck go away. There was only one way to rid himself of such things, and that was to just get on with what was causing him to be anxious.

His mother gave him a reassuring smile as she joined him in rising when Flitcroft appeared at the sitting room door.

"Whatever will be, will be," she whispered. "I shall not encourage or discourage any natural fondness for Miss Brinson."

But she would wish for there to be a natural fondness. As she had told him when he tracked her down after hearing about his sister's scheming to match him with Miss Brinson, her wish for his happiness was the motivation for all her machinations.

She wished for him to find a wife who would complement him and bring to his life the joy that his father had brought to hers.

However, she had also promised in that same conversation, that she would refrain from any attempt to convince him of the worth of Miss Brinson or any other female when they entered the season – well, she would refrain beginning then. She could not retract the opportunity she had already provided him by arranging for Miss Brinson to be entering his...

Thought left him as the very lady about whom he had been thinking floated into the room. Surely, she did not walk, for a creature such as she must have fairy wings. Hair the colour of newly spun flax was softly piled on her head. The bluest of eyes danced with pleasure as she greeted his sister. A hint of pink from the coolness of the day coloured her cheeks and the tip of her nose. It was a lovely shade against the clearness of her creamy complexion. If she had a few roses woven into her hair, she'd be precisely as delicate and beautiful as the teacup to which his sister had compared her.

"And this is my son, Frederick. Frederick, this

is my dear friend, Mrs. Brinson, and her daughter, Miss Brinson."

He blinked at his mother when she continued to look at him but remained silent. There was something he was supposed to do, but what was it? His mother tipped her head toward their guests while silently begging him to understand with her eyes.

Ah, that was it! With a less than proper bow, he mumbled something he hoped would sound like a greeting to Mrs. and Miss Brinson. It was not at all what he had prepared to say, but, at least, it was over. He should be able to gather his wits and proceed with life as always now. His heart should begin to calm, and the fog which had settled over his mind should lift, for the hardest part was the beginning. That was how it had always worked. Until now. His heart was still beating wildly, and his mind was still a jumble. Proper procedure. He just needed to follow proper procedure, and all would be well.

"You would probably like to be shown to your rooms before tea," he suggested. That was what one did when a guest arrived. First, you greeted them. Then, you allowed them to get settled, and finally, you offered refreshment.

"That is what Mother just said." Rosalie looked as if she was about to burst from the laughter she was suppressing.

Frederick looked from his sister to his mother and back. "Did she?" He had not heard her.

His sister nodded and pressed her lips together more firmly.

Well! This was a fine start to things!

"I apologize," he said to Mrs. Brinson, "I was distracted. There is a matter that needs my attention. If you will excuse me, I will go attend to it. I am sure my mother has this all well-in-hand." He bowed and beat what he hoped was not too hasty a retreat to his study where, after closing the door, he leaned against it and pulled in deep breaths. What an utter idiot! He thumped his head against the door. A mumbling, stumbling dimwit!

Pushing off the door, he crossed to his desk and dropped into his chair. How was he supposed to survive a visit not just from new acquaintance – for that is what the Brinsons were to him – but from a new acquaintance who rendered him speechless just to look at her.

"You have been through how many seasons?" he

directed the question to the empty chair in front of him.

"Five," he answered for the uncommunicative piece of furniture.

"And how many strangers have you asked to dance or take a drive?" He raised a brow and gave the chair an accusatory glare.

"A great number," he again answered for the chair.

"And how many drawing and music rooms have you sat in where you were required to speak like a rational creature to strangers?"

"You have not even counted them because they are so numerous," he replied in the chair's stead.

"So why are you so nervous about this young lady? She is just another debutante." He sighed – except she was not just another debutante whom he was meeting for the first time. Miss Brinson was Miss Lily, his sister's friend, to whom he had presented himself as less than astute before she had even stepped one foot inside his home. How could a brother not know that his sister was the person to whom a letter was addressed?

He dropped his head into his hands. He was a hopeless fool, and she was precisely the sort of young woman who would have captured his attention in a crowd of a thousand. The very sort of young lady he would wish to impress. He groaned. He was certain he had made an impression. Sadly, it was not a good one, and how did one correct that when he found her presence to be so discombobulating? There had to be a solution to his dilemma. He could not just hide in his study until the new year – even if that was presently what he wished to do. He would just have to put some thought into it. Maybe over a glass of port.

"Freddie?"

"What do you want?" he growled without looking up. He had heard the door open but had not particularly cared to see which servant had entered. And while his sister was not a servant, he still had no interest in looking at her as she was whom he was blaming for his current frustrations.

Slipper soft steps approached his desk.

"Mr. George."

Frederick's eyes grew wide and his heart threatened to race out of the safe confines of his chest in search of a safer place. Slowly he lifted his head. Where was his sister? He searched the room.

"Sally is just outside the door," Miss Brinson

explained. "If she hears your mother or mine, she will slip into the room so that all will be as proper as can be." She motioned to the chair he had only moments before been lecturing about his lack of ability to speak to a pretty young lady. "May I?"

He nodded and then sprang from his chair while he muttered an apology. He knew to stand when a lady entered a room. What had become of him? He shook his head and sighed. Had he ever been so dimwitted before?

"You may sit down," Miss Brinson said with a small laugh. "I am not easily offended."

"That is good," he muttered as he retook his seat. "I can be quite good at giving offense. Not that I mean to do so, of course."

"Of course."

Her smile was mesmerizing.

She ducked her head when he continued to stare at her, and he pulled his eyes away from her.

"I understand from your sister that she has played a bit of a prank on us."

His brow furrowed.

Miss Brinson leaned toward his desk and lowered her voice. "My letter about my mother."

Right!

"I have forgiven her, of course, and I thought it best if you and I dispensed directly with the awkwardness such a lark naturally arouses. I find that is usually best, do you not agree?"

"I would most likely agree if I could think. I seem to be short on that particular ability today."

She chuckled. "You do not lack wit, Mr. George, but then, your sister can be very droll, and she had told me that you were not without a sense of humor." She paused and looked down at her hands. "Which is why I was not afraid to write to you and her as I did."

"Then, as I suspected once my sister confessed her ploy to me, you did know it was me who had replied to your letter. Rosalie seemed to think you did not know from how, in your letter to her, you presented your suppositions about who had written to you."

"I did know it was your, but I was afraid you would read the second letter as you had the first. Therefore, I suggested that it was not you who had received the first letter." She shrugged. "I apologize for not just ending the charade. However, and I likely should not admit this, I was dreadfully curious to hear how you would respond to my reply."

Frederick sat back in his chair and just looked at her for a moment. Had she truly wished for a reply? It had not seemed so in her letter – not that her appearance of not wishing for a reply had stopped him from writing her a note. "What of your fear of scandal? Was that also manufactured?"

"No," she answered quickly and with some force.

"Would not a second letter from me to you create a greater chance of being discovered?" Perhaps that was what she had wanted. Perhaps she was just another scheming female. Heaven knows he was surrounded by enough of those!

She blinked. "I suppose it would, but that was not my intention."

"Are you certain?"

Her mouth dropped open. "I have no need to trap a husband! I am not that sort of lady!"

"I did not say you were." Had he? His right eye closed as he attempted to review his words.

"You most certainly did!" she assured him before he could replay their interaction. "How do I know that you were not hoping to force me into accepting you by writing to me in the first place?" She was standing in front of his desk, looking for all the world like she was about to stomp out of his study and close the door with a great deal of force.

"I was only clarifying."

She crossed her arms. "Clarifying whether or not I was a schemer!"

"Precisely. Clarifying –"

"So you did think I was a schemer!"

Oh! What was it with females and their ability to twist words and tie his mind and tongue in knots? His sister was an expert at just such a thing.

"I do not." He deliberately attempted to make his tone calming. However, it did not appear to be helping.

She uncrossed her arms and, placing her hands on his desk, leaned forward and glared down at him.

She was standing! He had done it again. He pushed up from his chair. Why could he not remember his manners?

"You just said that you were clarifying if I was a schemer."

"No, I did not. I just said that I was clarifying that you were not a schemer – not a schemer." He leaned toward her as he repeated himself. She smelled like – he drew in a deep breath and smiled. "Roses."

She blinked. "I beg your pardon?"

"You smell like roses. They are kind of an important thing around here. Roses seem to surround us here – in the linens, the dishware, the silver, and, of course, in the garden. And then there is my sister's name, as well as that of our home." His brow furrowed. "Why do you call my sister Sally?"

Miss Brinson's expression declared quite loudly that she thought he was not in possession of his faculties.

"Are you attempting to distract me from the fact that you thought I could be a schemer?"

Frederick shook his head and leaned just a bit closer to her. Roses were such a lovely fragrance. "No, though you are in here. Alone. With me. And that is of your own volition, so even if I did think you could be a schemer, which I do not, it is not without foundation."

"We are not alone. Your sister," she moved an inch closer to him, "is standing guard against a compromise."

"My sister would like nothing better than for me to be forced to marry." He swallowed as his eyes slipped to her pretty pink lips. "And I would like nothing better than to kiss you."

"That would be excessively scandalous."

Her lips tipped up at the corners into a teasing smile, but she did not move away from him.

"Perhaps," she continued with a flutter of her lashes much as his sisters did when she was being provoking, "it is you who is the schemer if you are thinking such thoughts?"

He smiled and shook his head. "You seem to be inviting me to act on my wishes. Are you certain you are not a schemer?"

Her smile faded and surprise settled in her eyes. "I... I was... until this moment, but now... well, now, I am not so certain." She drew and released a deliberate breath as if breathing for her was as challenging a thing as it was for him.

"Why is that?" he whispered. Her lips were so close.

"Because," her reply was tantalizingly breathy, "I would very much like for you to kiss me."

He leaned forward intent upon granting her wish and his own.

"Freddie."

He closed his eyes and groaned a mere breath

away from Miss Brinson's lips. "Could you not just wait outside the door for a moment longer?" he grumbled, causing both her and Miss Brinson to giggle – one with obvious amusement and the other nervously.

"I hear Mother, but if you would like me to leave again..." She pulled the door open.

"No!" He stood and straightened his jacket. He wished for a kiss but not at the expense of being discovered kissing the daughter of his mother's friend less than an hour after her arrival.

"Sit." He motioned to the chairs in front of his desk. "And please choose a topic of conversation that Mother will find acceptable and about which I might have a hope of participating in without causing offense."

Chapter 4

"Good morning, Miss Brinson," Frederick said as he passed her on the staircase where she was going up, and he was going down. "Have you broken your fast?"

It had been three days since Lily's arrival and so far, he had learned that she was an early riser, enjoyed playing cards in the evening, and almost always took a short walk in the morning before she had her breakfast.

"We have." She stopped two steps above where he had stopped.

He loved the way her eyes lit when she smiled. Her delight was never just confined to a small portion of face but seemed to fill her whole being.

"We?" he questioned, knowing full-well that she was referring to herself and his sister.

She giggled. "Sally and I."

"Did my sister abandon you?"

Miss Brinson shook her head. "I told her I was going up ahead of her because I fear I am much slower at getting ready for a ride than she is."

"You are going riding?"

"It was decided on our second turn of the garden this morning."

"It looks as if it is going to rain. Are you certain it is a good idea to go riding?"

Her eyes travelled up and down his attire. "It seems you think it is a good idea, for you appear to be dressed for a ride."

She had him there.

"I am not so delicate that a few smatterings of rain will wash me away," she added.

"Or into a sick bed?" That was the danger he feared. Rain did not usually wash people away unless they were standing near a flooded river or on the edge of an unstable ridge.

"I am nearly certain I will not succumb to illness if I get wet, for staying well is just a matter of becoming dry before one gets too chilled."

"Then you are staying near the house?"

Her lips pursed and her brow furrowed. "Where we ride is entirely up to your sister. Perhaps you should give her your instructions." She turned to leave him.

"Miss Brinson," he called after her, causing her to turn toward him again, "I do not mean to be demanding. I just do not wish for you to fall ill."

"Then, I thank you for your care, sir." She dipped a small curtsey and proceeded to climb the rest of the stairs, leaving him to descend to the floor below and seek out his sister in the dining rooms so that he might express his concern to her before he collected Chase and Cooper and set out to rout a few birds.

"Lily seems as smitten as Freddie does."

Frederick stopped outside the dining room where breakfast had been laid out, and, apparently, his sister was having a discussion with someone.

"It does seem to be going quite well. Better than I had hoped."

He shook his head. His mother and his sister were still at their games!

"And I have not had to do a thing to promote the match," his mother added.

"Lilith is not usually so compliant."

Mrs. Brinson was also complicit?

"Neither is Frederick," his mother replied with a laugh.

"Do you think she met him by now?" His sister asked. "Do you think it is safe for me to go get my things for riding?"

"Do you know where he will be riding?" his mother asked.

"Lily was to ask him."

Fred's eyebrows rose nearly to his hairline. It seemed it was not only birds being hunted today, but also him! Sorrow as grey as the darkest cloud in midwinter settled over him for it seemed Miss Brinson was not an innocent victim of the scheming ladies in the dining room. She was a participant. Why? There was no need to arrange meetings. He had almost kissed her after her arrival for heaven's sake! If that had not told her that he found her compelling, then she was far stupider than he imagined anyone could be.

He blew out a breath, attempting to rid himself of the despondence he felt before he took the remaining five steps into the dining room and put an end to both their and his hopes for him and Miss Brinson.

"It looks like rain," he said upon entering the

room. "I will see that there is a bird or two for dinner, Mother, and attempt to avoid the worst of the weather." He looked at his sister. "I told Miss Brinson that it was perhaps not wise to ride today. I hope you will not put yourself or your friend in harm's way for some stratagem." He bowed to the three startled ladies before him and took his leave before any of them could find their tongues.

He would not be part of some scheme. Anger mingled with pain in his breast.

He whistled and was rewarded with the sound of dogs rousing from their repose and scampering down the hall toward him. He scratched the ears of both when they caught up to him. If it were not for the fact that Chase and Cooper needed a good run and scrounge through the fields, he would just ask Mr. Morris to see to the birds for dinner.

"Freddie."

He pretended to not hear his sister.

"Freddie!" her voice grew louder, and her steps became more hurried.

He spun toward her. "What?"

She drew back at his tone.

"I have things to do, Rosalie."

Her brow furrowed, and for a moment, he felt

like a cad for having spoken so harshly to her. However, the remorse was quickly washed away when he remembered why he was put out with her.

Cautiously, she joined him at the bottom of the staircase which led up to the bedrooms, just where it turned to make the descent from the first floor to the ground floor.

"You seemed out of sorts, and I was concerned."

"Are you truly concerned for me?"

Confusion etched her features as she nodded.

"Does it matter to you at all that I would like to find my own wife?"

Her eyes grew wide, and she swallowed.

"And I think I should like a wife," he continued, "who does not need to be convinced to like me."

"It is not like that," she protested.

"I heard you and Mother just now." He turned from her. "Mr. Westwood is joining me for my hunt. Should I bring him home to call on you?"

"No!" She snatched at his elbow but missed.

"Perhaps I will do it anyway." He was a step below her. "I only want what is best for you."

She gasped.

"Or perhaps you could arrange for him to court your friend since I have no intention of doing so.

There are too many scheming women around this house as it is. I do not need another one!" No matter how pretty she was or how much he enjoyed spending time with her.

"Freddie, please. I can explain."

"Oh, I am sure you can, and I, like a fool, would believe you – again." He whistled to the dogs who were sitting at his sister's feet. Those beasts loved her more than chasing a rabbit down a hole. "Chase. Cooper. Come."

"Go on," his sister whispered. "And give him a kiss for me."

Ouch! His heart clenched at her words and hurt tone. However, he was not going to apologize for he had every right to be angry. She and the other conniving females in this house were the ones who needed to apologize. He was perfectly capable of selecting a wife on his own. He did not need them to push one at him.

~*~*~

"I have half a mind to take your gun from you before you do damage to something of value," Luke Westwood teased Frederick an hour later.

They had been taking turns shooting the birds that Cooper and Chase sent flying. Luke had hit every one of the birds at which he had aimed. Frederick had not been as successful.

"You have not shot so poorly since you were ten," Luke added.

"I am distracted."

"I had noticed. Your ability to keep up your side of a conversation has been little better than your aim. Do you care to tell me about your distraction?"

"No." Frederick lifted his gun and watched the sky above where Chase was barking. However, nothing flew out of the brush.

"It is likely a hare," Luke said. "Lower your weapon and tell me what has you in such a state. You only wanted three birds and that is what you have even if it took you twice as many shots to get them than it normally does. There is no need to keep shooting. Let the dogs play."

Frederick did as his friend suggested while considering the cause of his current disagreeable frame of mind. "We have guests at Rose Hall." One very pretty one who he had thought liked him of her own accord but apparently did not.

"Yes, you told me you were going to have visitors. Are they unpleasant?"

"No." Mrs. and Miss Brinson had been all that was agreeable. Of course, that was likely just part of their machinations. "They are too pleasant."

His friend let out a surprised laugh. "I am not certain I understand how guests can be too pleasant or how that can cause a person to be as disgruntled as you are today."

Frederick blew out a breath and launched into the problem with his guests. "Miss Brinson is beautiful."

His friend's eyebrows rose in interest.

"I honestly could not form a coherent thought or follow a conversation when I met her." He swung up onto his horse.

Luke whistled as he checked to make sure his birds were secured before mounting his own horse.

"And she is interesting – not just pretty."

"So, then what is the problem?"

"My mother. And hers. And my sister. And Miss Brinson herself." He shook his head. "It seems the whole visit was arranged so that Miss Brinson could become Mrs. George."

"Ah. I see, and you are dissatisfied with the fact that your mother and sister, as well as your guests, have presented a beautiful, interesting lady to you as a possible wife."

Frederick scowled. When put like that, it did not seem so very bad, but it was. It truly was, or, at least, it most certainly felt like it was.

"Do I strike you as so desperate as to need assistance in finding a lady and securing her affections?"

Luke shook his head. "You have never wanted for ladies willing to fall at your feet. Of course, half of them were swooning over your dashing good looks."

Despite his foul mood, Frederick chuckled.

"And the other half were swooning over Rose Hall and your bank account. Not that I can blame them. I would find myself feeling a bit lightheaded over the idea of securing your fortune."

Again, Frederick chuckled.

"Yes, well, I should like to be desired for more than my appearance or wealth."

"So fastidious!" Luke cried. "I do think one can be too choosy." He clapped his friend on the shoulder. "Are you certain that this Miss Brinson has no interest in you?"

"That is just the thing. I do not know. At first, I thought she might, but then, I heard our mothers and my sister discussing their scheme." He shook his head. "I even asked Miss Brinson if she was a schemer, and she proclaimed she was not."

And, fool that he was, he had believed her, just as he had trusted his mother and sister when they said they would not play at matchmaking while the Brinsons were in residence.

He looked up to the sky. "We should head home. Those clouds are not growing any less grey."

"And she is still participating in a ploy to snare you after you asked her such a thing?"

"It appears she is."

"I cannot believe you asked her that." Luke was still looking appalled.

"There was a letter, and my sister – suffice it to say, my sister was arranging things before Miss Brinson arrived and it appeared both Miss Brinson and me were the victims of her plotting."

The appalled look had shifted to confusion on his friend's face.

"Miss Brinson asked me the same." And then, he had almost kissed her.

His friend's confused expression had not softened, but thankfully, he seemed willing to let the explanation stay as it was in favour of pursuing other inquiries. "Is she poor?"

Frederick shook his head. "I do not think so. Why?"

Luke tipped his head and looked at Frederick as if he was missing something obvious. Of course, Frederick had no idea what it was.

"Miss Brinson is both beautiful enough to render a fellow speechless and not poor?"

Frederick nodded. That was an accurate assessment of Miss Brinson.

"And yet, after you insulted her by accusing her of being a schemer, she still wishes to pursue you?"

"So, it seems."

"Why?" Luke had stopped riding.

"I am certain I could not tell you," Frederick said in answer to his friend's expectant look.

"You, my friend, are beyond hope at times. You performed well on all your exams in school. How can you not figure out that Miss Brinson might be interested in you?"

"I do not see how that is easily seen."

"If she is beautiful and not poor, what do you think her chances are of securing a husband during her first season?" He paused as if waiting for Frederick to respond but replied to his own question before Frederick could do more than open his mouth. "I should think she would be betrothed before the daffodils are in bloom. She does not *need* you to accept her, Fred. She *wants* you to accept her."

"That cannot be." Could it?

"Think what you will, but I'd put money on it that I am right." He shook his head and chuckled. "Do you think she would be willingly participating in a scheme which could end up with her married to you if she did not want to be tied to you – especially since she does not need your money and is not lacking in the beauty necessary to secure an offer or two in town?"

He had not thought of it in such a way.

"Women scheme, just as men do, to get what they want."

He had to admit that was true.

"Do you want to come to Rose Hall for tea?" Frederick offered as they drew close to where they must part.

Luke shook his head. "I have birds to deliver to my cook. Though I will admit the thought of being introduced to a beautiful lady is tempting."

That was not surprising. His friend was fond of admiring beautiful ladies.

"Well, it is unfortunate that you cannot join me because I told my sister I would bring you home to court her."

Luke guffawed. "Poor Rosalie must have really infuriated you for you to make such a threat."

She had. She had promised not to interfere, and she had, which made him feel quite inadequate. What a sorry excuse! Was he so arrogant as to lash out at someone he loved because his pride had been wounded? As disconcerting it was to admit, it seemed he was.

"You are not so very bad a fellow – handsome, well-set with land and funds, and as amiable a chap as I ever met. I do not know why she considers courting you such a horrid idea."

Luke shrugged. "It is likely because I am like a brother to her."

"Perhaps," Frederick muttered, though he doubted that was it. "Do you know Miss Brinson calls her Sally?"

"Sally?" Luke repeated as he pulled his collar a bit higher to ward off the wind which was picking up. "It suits her."

"That is just what Miss Brinson said when I asked about it! That was not the only reason she gave, however. There was also the fact that Rosie as a particularly familiar name would not do since it reminded Miss Brinson of her grandmother's horse, and Ros was not soft enough to suit." Even now he could picture Miss Brinson sitting in front of his desk with her cheeks still flushed from nearly kissing him and explaining her reasons for the name she had chosen for her friend when his mother had popped her head into his study to inform him that tea was waiting.

He was an idiot.

What did it matter if it had been arranged for him to meet Miss Brinson or if he had been promoted to her? He wanted her to sit in front of his desk and speak to him so candidly again. She was fascinating and charming, and he truly wished to know if they would suit. Perhaps it was as Luke had said. Perhaps Miss Brinson had gone along with her mother's scheme because she wanted to do so.

There was only one way to discover the answer.

"Give my greetings to your mother and sister," Luke called as he angled his horse towards his home.

"I will," Frederick assured him.

"I will call to meet your guests before too long." And with a nod of his head, Luke took his leave.

"Chase, Cooper! Time to go home to Rosalie." With tails wagging, the dogs came bounding out of the field to join him on the road. Cooper barked and ran after Chase who was ahead of them all, as he often was. Frederick nudged his horse to a gallop, for he was just as anxious as his dogs to get home so he could attempt to make things right.

Chapter 5

"It might be best if we do leave. It was not my intention to cause strife in your family, Flora."

"It is not your fault, Violet. I knew that it was a risk to even present the idea to you, but you can see how they would suit, can you not?" There was almost a begging tone to his mother's words that smote his conscience with a resounding thwack.

"Perfectly. It is as if they were designed for each other," Mrs. Brinson sounded as despondent as his mother.

What a mess he had made of things. Christmas was soon upon them, and instead of festooning the house in cheer and joy and lifting it out of the dreariness of midwinter, he had managed to settle it into the bleakness of this time of the year.

He peeked through the gap left in the not all the way secured drawing room door. He could see his

mother and her friend, but his sister and Miss Brinson were nowhere to be seen. He looked down at
the dogs who were at his heels.

"Find Rosalie," he whispered. "Go on. Where is
Rosalie?"

Chase was off with his nose to the floor sniffing
from one side of the hall to the other, while
Cooper sat with his tongue hanging out and a
happy look on his face watching Chase. Then, as
Chase's head popped up and he eyed the stairs,
Cooper dashed from where he was sitting and up
the staircase. Frederick chuckled and followed.
Rosalie must be in her room. However, his dogs did
not stop at Rosalie's door but proceeded to the one
Frederick knew had been assigned to Miss Brinson.

He could not go there. Even to knock on her
door would not be proper. He ran a hand through
his hair. How was he supposed to beg his sister for
forgiveness if he could not knock and ask to be
seen by her?

Cooper barked. Chase pawed the door, sniffed
along the bottom of the door, and pawed the door
again while Cooper added a second bark. There
was a rattle of the doorknob that caused both dogs

to stand alert, save for the wag of their tails. And then, the door opened.

"Rosalie," Frederick called. But it was not Rosalie. It was Miss Brinson who had opened the door. "Is my sister in there?" he asked. Heavens! Miss Brinson did not look well. Her hair was somewhat of a mess and her nose was red. "Are you well?" He took two steps toward her door before he stopped himself.

"I am quite well," Miss Brinson said curtly, stepping to the side to allow Cooper and Chase to enter the room. "Sally, do you wish to speak to your brother?" Miss Brinson turned back to him. "I am sorry, there is no one here who wishes to see you." And with that, and a cool look, she closed the door.

Well, that put a wrinkle in things. Again, he ran his hand through his hair as he stood there looking at that closed door for a full minute before he headed toward his own room.

By the time he had divested himself of his riding clothes and donned a new set, he had a plan formulated. With a sense of urgency, he hurried to his study.

"Were you successful?" His mother asked as he

entered the drawing room. He had thought to go to his study through its main door which attached to the corridor but had elected to pass through this room instead so that he might see his mother.

"I was. Cook is in possession of three birds." He stopped at her chair and, cupping her face in his hands, kissed her forehead. "I was abominable," he whispered.

Though her lips smiled, her eyes filled with tears.

"I know," he added. "And I love you, too." He kissed her forehead again. "Now, I have some business that demands my attention."

He bowed to Mrs. Brinson. "Good day, madame. I do hope you are finding the light good for your needlework. If not, I can move the chair closer to the window or bring a lamp. The clouds are not allowing for much sunlight today, I am afraid."

"I have not found it too dark yet," she assured him. "But it is kind of you to offer."

He nodded and left both his mother and Mrs. Brinson staring after him in silence for the second time that day. Thankfully, this time, such a look was not inspired by poor behavior. It should likely make him just as dissatisfied with himself that his good behaviour was something which warranted such surprise, but it did not since he knew that his current behaviour was the stark opposite of his previous behavior and therefore, should make anyone pause.

He settled into the large leather chair behind his desk and took out his writing set, carefully, opening the lid and placing the items within in the exact places where he wanted them. Then, with a deep cleansing breath drawn and released, he dipped his pen in the ink and set about his purpose.

Miss Lily,

I apologize for not having responded to your last missive. I happened upon some startling information on the day on which I received it which prevented me from sending you my response. You see, we are not complete strangers, or more precisely, you were not to remain a stranger to me. It seems you are a friend of my sister.

It may seem strange to you that a gentleman would not know the names of his sister's friends, especially when he is the guardian of that sister. However, I have not been her guardian for very long. My mother and father have always seen to her needs and attended her at functions in town during her season. However, that shall fall to me this year, now that our period of mourning is over.

This admission will likely paint me in a poor light, but based on what you said in your first misdirected letter, which it seems was not so very misdirected, I think you can understand my wishing to avoid the matchmaking schemes of my mother during the season. Because of that desire, I would often spend more time than not with my friends rather than my family.

May I share a secret? I regret having done so. There was so much I could have learned from my father. However, I did not realize my time to learn from him was to be so brief. I hope that you can bear up under your mother's machinations better than I have mine. I become quite disagreeable when pressed to call upon this lady or that because my mother thinks they would be a good match. I would prefer to be my own man.

Today, I became so out of sorts that I spoke quite harshly to my sister about not just her but also my mother and our guests. It was quite ungentlemanly of me, and now, when I am feeling very grieved over my words, my sister will not see me – and rightly so! I deserve her censure.

Since your last letter, we have had guests arrive at Rose Hall – my mother's dear friend, Mrs. Brinson, and her daughter. Miss Lily, you will likely not believe me when I tell you just how beautiful Miss Brinson is. She quite took my breath, as well as my ability to think rationally, away just by entering the room. Such lightness of spirit as shines in her eyes is entrancing. Her features are as delicate as fine porcelain. I dare say her slippers nary wear out as she does not walk on the earth as we mortals do, but she floats.

You are likely laughing at so maudlin a description, but I have not finished.

Not only is she a fairy goddess in appearance, but she is also fascinating. We have not known each other long, but there has not yet been an instance of my needing to feign interest in anything she says. She is well-versed in many things and does not – thank God! – confine her topics of conversation to the mundane and safe things of life as many do.

I fear I may have lost my heart to her, though at present, my greater fear is that I shall never be given the opportunity to discover if she might one day allow me to hold her heart as she holds mine, for, as I mentioned above, I have behaved most grievously.

I wonder if I might impose upon you for a bit of advice, for I am uncertain how to proceed with Miss Brinson. If it were you whom I had accused of being a schemer after your telling me that you were not one, how might I atone for such a sin?

I do hope you will honor me with a reply even if it could be considered scandalous if the letter should fall into the hands of another.

With trembling hands and a fragile and contrite heart, I am...

Yours,

F.B. George

Once the ink was dry, Frederick carefully folded the letter and wrote *Miss Lily, Rose Hall, Second Floor, Third Door on the Right* on the outside of the missive before dribbling sealing wax onto the flap and pressing his ring into the wax. When the wax was firm, he rang for the butler and instructed him that the envelope was to be discreetly delivered. Not a soul was to know that such a letter had ever been written.

And then, he waited. He paced his study from desk to door and back, adding in a circuit of that large piece of furniture for a bit of variety. She had not sent the letter back unopened, so he dared to hope she had read it and not just consigned it to the fire with its seal unbroken.

He was just beginning to think he should take himself to the billiard's room to knock a few balls around when there was a soft knock on his study door followed by that door pushing open slowly as if the person opening it was not sure that it was the thing to do.

"You may enter," he encouraged.

"Are you certain you wish it?" Rosalie asked.

He crossed the room in four large steps and wrapped her in his arms. "Can you forgive me?"

"If you can forgive me."

"For what?"

"Interfering. I should have listened to you and respected your wishes. However, when Lily asked me if I would help her capture your attention, I could not resist."

He squeezed her more tightly which made her gasp as if she were being suffocated. "Please do not break me," she said with a laugh.

"Never," he promised before releasing her. "I am sure I could not find a sister I could tolerate any better than you," he teased before growing serious. "I should have let you explain yourself. Apparently, according to Mr. Westwood, scheming is a part of life and does not always have a dire motive such as those I love thinking I am lacking in some way."

"Oh, Freddie, no! You lack nothing."

"That is patently false, my dear sister. I know I lack a great many things such as patience and the ability to think things through as well as I should at times – such as today." He motioned to the chair in front of his desk.

She shook her head. "I have only come to give you this." She held his letter, with its broken seal, out to him. "What you wrote is beautiful," she whispered as he took it.

His heart seemed to have jumped to his throat, making it impossible for him to do anything more than nod mutely at his sister while turning the letter over in his hand and beginning to unfold it. There at the bottom of his letter was a short note written in Lily's feminine hand.

Mr. George,

I find your lack of adherence to propriety in sending this letter to me after I specifically scolded you about writing to me in my previous missive to be endearing. Your Miss Brinson is a fortunate lady. If I were you, I would write her a letter revealing your heart to her as you have to me in the letter above. I would do this daily if need be until she relented and was unable to deny me any longer.

However, if I were Miss Brinson and you were as

charming and handsome as my dear friend Sally's brother, as your letter suggests you are, I would not waste a moment in allowing you to court me. I should not even fear my mother's machinations if I knew that they would lead to you.

May you find your heart has not been lost in vain,
Miss Lily

Could one smile more broadly or look more like a smitten fool than he was looking right now? He glanced up at his sister, but she was not there.

"Mr. George," the beautiful fairy goddess before his desk whispered.

"You will give me a chance?" he asked as he moved around to stand in front of his desk and next to her.

"I might be a schemer." Her eyes sparkled, and her lips pursed as if holding back a smile.

"I do not care," he replied. "As long as your scheming leads you to me and me to you, I do not care." He took her hands and pulled her a step towards him. Her nose was still a little red as were her eyes. "Are you well?"

"I am now," she said, pulling her hands away from him and wrapping her arms round his neck. "But I was not when I heard you say you would never court me, for I have never longed for something so much as I longed for you to court me."

His arms encircled her waist and pulled her close. "If either of our mothers were to see us like this, we would be bound to each other for more than a courtship," he cautioned.

She smiled as his head dipped towards her. "Yes, I have thought of that." Her eyes darted toward the door to the drawing room just as it opened while her hands drew him the rest of the way to her.

As he pressed his lips to hers and her body to his, he willingly allowed himself to fall victim to a matchmaking scheme which enveloped not only his senses but also his very soul. The lady in his arms was and always would be his Lily – a bright spot in his life not only when the sun shone brightly on a glorious summer day but also when the clouds hung low as they often did in midwinter.

Before You Go

If you enjoyed this book, be sure to let others know by leaving a review.

~*~*~

Want to know when other books in this series will be available?

You can always know what's new with my books by subscribing to my mailing list.

(There will, of course, be a thank you gift for joining because I think my readers are awesome!)

Book News from Leenie Brown

(bit.ly/LeenieBBookNews)

~*~*~

Turn the page to read an excerpt of another one of Leenie's books

A Scandal in Springtime Excerpt

If you look at my catalogue of published titles, you will notice that I like to combine my love of sweet Regency romance with my love of Jane Austen's books and characters. I especially love writing stories for Miss Austen's secondary characters. One example of such a book that gives a happily ever after to a lesser character from Pride and Prejudice is A Scandal in Springtime. This book is book three in my Darcy Family Holidays series and stars Kitty Bennet. Below is the first chapter of that book.

CHAPTER 1

Kitty Bennet paused at the case containing the lace and brooches. There was a piece of lace intricately woven with leaves and flowers swirling along the edge and filling in the body which she would dearly like to purchase so that she could add it to her scarf. Just on the shelf above the lace was a brooch comprised of many tiny pearls which would be perfect for holding the scarf in place.

Perhaps next week when Uncle gave her the allowance her father had sent to him, she would have enough to purchase those two items so that she could wear them to church on Easter Sunday.

"Catherine."

Kitty jumped, her cheeks warming with embarrassment. "Forgive me, Uncle. I was distracted." Thankfully, even though her uncle had used her full name, he did not look put out. "That brooch is just so pretty," she added as she hurried to catch up to him.

"I am certain it is," he replied. "Although I am certain your aunt would know better, my dear."

"Do you think we can bring Aunt with us next time?"

The establishment through which they were walking was a new store that her uncle had said was nearly ready to open. And it appeared he was right, for the cases and shelves were filled with goods, the windows were being washed, and the floor looked as if it had already been polished.

Her uncle chuckled. "I am quite certain your aunt will demand it."

Kitty was not yet completely comfortable with her aunt and uncle – at least, not in the way her older sisters had always been. Jane and Elizabeth were always so at ease whenever the Gardiners visited Longbourn, but that was likely because they had spent so many visits with the Gardiners in town. However, now that her older sisters were married, that was about to change.

She and Mary were to take turns visiting their relations, for their mother hoped that in sending them to London, her remaining unattached daughters might happen upon some nice young gentlemen who would marry them and relieve Mrs. Bennet of two more worries. There was no more significant worry for a mother than to see her daughters well-cared-for. That is what Mama had always said.

Kitty put all thoughts of scarves and brooches, as well as handsome young gentlemen, away as she stood behind her uncle while he knocked at the door to the store's office before opening it when someone inside called *come in.*

"Mr. Gardiner, it is good to see you. With what can I help you?"

"Not a thing, Mr. Durward," her uncle replied. "My wife insisted that we deliver a basket of muffins to you as a gift of goodwill for the success of your store."

He looked at Kitty. "The basket," he whispered.

"I do apologize." Her cheeks burned once again with embarrassment, and she spared a quick glance for Mr. Durward. "I was distracted." How could she not be? The gentleman standing in front of the desk, the one who was not Mr. Durward, was far too attractive not to be distracting.

Her uncle chuckled. "This store seems to have that effect on you."

He took the basket from her and placed it on the desk. "There is one case containing brooches that my niece found of great interest. I think you will have a sale on your first day even if no one else enters the store."

"I am happy to hear it," Mr. Durward said with a friendly smile for Kitty. "Please be seated," he offered.

"I am afraid we are not able to stay today," Mr. Gardiner replied. "There are a few other errands which need our attention. However, Kitty and I wanted to see the basket delivered first." His brow furrowed. "I seem to have forgotten that you have not yet met my niece. This pretty young lady is Miss Catherine Bennet, and she is our houseguest for a few weeks this spring. Kitty, this is Mr. Durward and one of his partners, Mr. Waller."

Kitty dipped a curtsey. "It is lovely to meet you and to see your store. It is very well done up."

"Thank you," Mr. Durward replied, and Kitty found herself compelled once again to remove her eyes from Mr. Waller — handsome, tall Mr. Waller with his golden hair and piercing blue eyes.

"Have you settled into the apartment above?" Mr. Gardiner asked.

Mr. Waller lived here? Kitty's heart sank a trifle at the thought. She probably should not like him if he lived above a store. Mama might not approve.

"I have, and I have even employed a maid and a cook. It is a luxury I have not allowed myself until now. However, I think, even with the extra expense, I shall still be able to save the money I need to secure my future."

That seemed a funny thing for a gentleman to say, and Kitty wondered what it meant. However, she knew better than to ask. It was not right to be nosey, and while in town, Kitty intended to behave properly.

Here, she was not Lydia's sister. Indeed, she was no one's sister when she was alone with her aunt and uncle even if she still had to be Elizabeth's sister when she was attending one function or another with the Darcy's. However, it was not so bad to say that Mrs. Darcy was her sister for Mrs. Darcy was married. But Miss Kitty Bennet was not.

She was still thinking about how delightful it was to not be anyone's sister and have all the beaux to herself when her uncle said her full name – *Catherine* – once again.

"Forgive me," she muttered. She needed to work on not looking like such a distracted fool – especially when in the presence of a very handsome gentleman like Mr. Waller. At least, she had not been caught admiring him.

"It was a pleasure to meet you, Mr. Durward, Mr. Waller," Kitty said in parting before preceding her uncle out of the office as he motioned for her to do.

"You are excessively distracted today," her uncle said as he wrapped her arm around his.

He was likely holding her hand on his arm to

keep her from peering into any more of the cases. It was a far more enjoyable way to have one's attention focused than scolding or teasing ever was. She liked how her uncle patted her hand as if he enjoyed having her at his side.

"I get lost in my thoughts sometimes," she admitted.

"And are these happy thoughts?"

She nodded. "Sometimes they are about real life and other times they are about... well... a great number of things that are not real at all."

"Stories?"

She looked at her uncle. He seemed the sort of gentleman who would not make fun of a lady for being less intelligent than Elizabeth, but she was not entirely sure he would not tease her for dreaming up stories in her head. However, she nodded anyway. Lying was not proper, and in town, she was attempting to be proper.

"Would you like for me to stop at my warehouse and pick up a notebook for you in which to write these stories?"

"You would do that?" How shocking!

He nodded.

"You do not think it foolish of me to think up stories?"

He shook his head and held the door open for her. "Not at all. I quite enjoy reading."

So did Papa, but Kitty could not imagine him not saying writing stories was foolish. Stories did not seem to her to be scholarly enough to garner her father's approval. "They are very fanciful."

She waited for her uncle to change his mind about her thinking up stories, but he paid her no mind.

"We will be going to my warehouse," he told the driver before helping her into the carriage. "You do want the notebook, do you not?"

Kitty snapped her mouth closed and smiled while nodding. He was not going to change his mind. No wonder Elizabeth and Jane liked visiting Aunt and Uncle Gardiner so much!

"Uncle," she said as he took his seat, "I know it is not polite to inquire after things which are not my business, but I was wondering if it were possible for you to explain to me what Mr. Waller meant about saving to secure his future."

"Ah." Her uncle gave her a knowing look. "I am afraid that young man is well on his way to being married. He has only to earn enough money to please the young lady's father."

"Oh." That was disappointing. He was very handsome.

"I am sorry," Uncle Gardiner whispered.

"As am I," Kitty admitted. "His eyes are very blue."

Her uncle chuckled. "They are. However, I am certain you will meet with many handsome gentlemen while you are in town. Did you not dance with several when you attended that ball with Elizabeth?"

"Oh, I danced nearly every set and several of my partners were very handsome." She sighed. "However, none of them had eyes as blue as Mr. Waller's." She looked out the window at the passing buildings. Nor did any of them have hair the colour of spun gold.

"There is more to finding a good match than the colour of a gentleman's eyes," her uncle cautioned.

Kitty sighed. "I know. I must also consider his fortune."

"And his character," her uncle added with a raised brow. "No matter what your mother might

tell you, a handsome character is far more important than a handsome fortune or face."

"Of course," she said quickly, her gaze dropping
from looking at her uncle to her clasped hands.

"I am not reprimanding," Uncle Gardiner said
softly. "At least, I am not reprimanding you. Your
mother, however..." He chuckled. "She has raised
five lovely daughters and prepared them quite well
to oversee a household, but..." He paused. "Thinking deeply was never one of her strengths, and I
fear, that in her exuberance to see you married to
a husband who can keep you in fine dresses, she
may have forgotten to instruct you about the qual-
ities beyond face and fortune which qualify a gentleman as a good choice."

Kitty tipped her head and thought about that for
a while. What had her mother taught her about
how to choose a proper husband other than to seek
one who was handsome and had a good income?
Her eyebrows rose. Very little.

"I suppose he should be amiable," she said to her
uncle. Mama did like agreeable gentlemen such as
Mr. Bingley.

"That is a good quality," her uncle agreed.
"Although amiability might be hidden at first."

Kitty nodded. "Like it was with Mr. Darcy."

Her uncle chuckled but did not disagree.

"Is there anything else you think a gentleman should be?" he asked.

She pulled her bottom lip between her teeth and sighed as she studied her gloved fingers. "I am not sure I know," she admitted with a shrug. "I wish for a handsome and amiable husband who has a good income."

The carriage began to slow. They were nearly to the warehouse.

"Those are excellent things for which to wish, but do not forget to find a gentleman who respects you and is kind."

"Oh, yes!" Why had she not thought of that? Of course, she did not want a husband who would make fun of her. Heaven knows she had endured enough of that in her life!

"And he should love you with his whole heart – to the point of death should he be separated from you."

Kitty blinked. She might have expected to hear such a statement from her aunt, but not from her uncle. He was a man. Men did not speak of such things. Did they?

"I see I have startled you," her uncle said. "I did not intend for my words to make you feel uneasy. I was just imagining what I would say to Priscilla if she were old enough to be seeking a husband."

He was thinking of her as his daughter? The idea wrapped around her, warm and comfortable, like a blanket made from the softest wool.

"At the risk of startling you more, that is how I feel about your aunt."

"It is?"

"Absolutely. I would be lost without her."

Oh, that was a very lovely thing! Kitty would most certainly like to marry a gentleman who felt that way about her.

"Then," Kitty said as the carriage door opened, "I suppose I must find a husband who is very much like you."

Acknowledgements

There are many who have had a part in the creation of these stories. My critique buddies have read and commented on it. My editors have proofread for grammatical errors and plot holes. My boys and husband have not read the story and most likely never will. However, their encouragement and belief in my ability, as well as their patience when I became cranky or when supper was late or the groceries ran low, was invaluable.

And so, I would like to say *thank you* to Zoe, Rose, Betty, Kristine, Ben, and Kyle. I feel blessed through your help, support, and understanding.

I have not listed my dear husband in the above group because, to me, he deserves his own special thank you, for without his somewhat pushy insistence that I start sharing my writing, none of my writing goals and dreams would have been met.

Other Leenie B Books

You can find all of Leenie's books at this link
bit.ly/LeenieBBooks
where you can explore the collections below

~*~

Other Pens, Mansfield Park

~*~

Touches of Austen Collection

~*~

Dash of Darcy and Companions Collection

~*~

Marrying Elizabeth Series

~*~

Willow Hall Romances

~*~

The Choices Series

~*~

Darcy Family Holidays

~*~

Darcy and... An Austen-Inspired Collection

About the Author

Leenie Brown has always been a girl with an active imagination, which, while growing up, was both an asset, providing many hours of fun as she played out stories, and a liability, when her older sister and aunt would tell her frightening tales. At one time, they had her convinced Dracula lived in the trunk at the end of the bed she slept in when visiting her grandparents!

Although it has been years since she cowered in her bed in her grandparents' basement, she still has an imagination which occasionally runs away with her, and she feeds it now as she did then — by reading!

Her heroes, when growing up, were authors, and the worlds they painted with words were (and still are) her favourite playgrounds! Now, as an adult, she spends much of her time in the Regency world, playing with the characters from her favourite Jane Austen novels and those of her own creation.

When she is not traipsing down a trail in an attempt to keep up with her imagination, Leenie resides in the beautiful province of Nova Scotia with her two sons and her very own Mr. Brown (a wonderful mix of all the best of Darcy, Bingley, and Edmund with a healthy dose of the teasing Mr. Tilney and just a dash of the scolding Mr. Knightley).

Connect with Leenie

E-mail:
LeenieBrownAuthor@gmail.com
Facebook:
www.facebook.com/LeenieBrownAuthor
Blog:
leeniebrown.com
Patreon:
https://www.patreon.com/LeenieBrown
Subscribe to Leenie's Mailing List:
Book News from Leenie Brown
(bit.ly/LeenieBBookNews)